287

1.50
70787

Harlequin Presents...

ANNE MATHER

fallen angel

D0048176

A Message from Janet Dailey to all Harlequin Readers:

In the month of May, Pocket Books, a division of Simon & Schuster, will publish a brand new novel by me entitled "Touch the Wind." I want all Harlequin readers to be aware that "Touch the Wind" is a more dramatic and compelling love story than a typical Harlequin, hence the change to a different publisher.

It is a contemporary love-adventure novel set in the Sierra Madre range of Mexico. Although there is a degree of violence in it and some slightly risqué love scenes, I have been told I may never again create a hero as intriguing and compelling as Ràfaga.

I know there are many of you who enjoy the stories that I have had in the Harlequin Presents series. It was not and is not my intention to offend any of you Harlequin readers with this new novel. To those of you who do read "Touch the Wind," I hope you find it to be an exciting and beautiful love story. I believe it is, although it is stronger than a Harlequin.

And I especially want to thank Harlequin and Mills & Boon for their support and encouragement in my venture into another field of writing. I realize Harlequin has its standards to maintain and could not, in good conscience, publish "Touch the Wind."

I enjoy writing Harlequin romances and will continue to write the kind of romances you readers enjoy as well. Besides, I still have twenty-one more States to go before I have a Harlequin romance set in every State.

Thank you and wish me luck on "Touch the Wind"!

Janet Dailey

Other titles by

ANNE MATHER
IN HARLEQUIN PRESENTS

Other titles by

ANNE MATHER
IN HARLEQUIN ROMANCES

◆

ANNE MATHER

fallen angel

Harlequin Books

TORONTO • LONDON • NEW YORK • AMSTERDAM
SYDNEY • HAMBURG • PARIS

Harlequin Presents edition published May 1979
ISBN 0-373-70787-8

Original hardcover edition published in 1978
by Mills & Boon Limited

CHAPTER ONE

JASON did not like London. He had not liked it when he was a student, and he liked it even less now. The crowded thoroughfares, all confusingly one way, the noise of the traffic, the sickly smell of diesel; all these things combined to make him yearn for the open spaces of his *estancia*; though it must be added that anyone observing his tall, immaculately-suited figure and darkly cynical features would never have suspected he felt more at home on the *pampa*.

It was strange, he reflected, when he had been born and brought up in England, albeit in the care of the local council, that he should feel more at ease in the South American republic where he had his home. The well-trammelled spaces of his fatherland held no interest for him, and as soon as he had obtained the engineering degree he had worked for, he left for more adventurous climes. But building bridges in Australia or pipelines in the Middle East soon began to pall, however, and because the money was good he joined a mercenary force fighting in Central Africa. But even money would not compensate for the lack of self-respect he felt facing a barefoot enemy, equipped with only the meanest kind of ammunition, with weaponry of the most sophisticated kind. He left for America with funds to pay the deposit on some land of his own, and succeeded only in blowing it all in on a speculative land deal that left him broke and jobless.

And that was how he met Charles Durham ...

Jason moved to the window of his hotel suite now and surveyed the busy street several floors below without enthusiasm. Was it really fifteen years since that bar-room brawl? He could hardly credit it. And yet so much had hap-

pened in the years since, he should not find it so difficult to
believe.

Durham was an archaeologist, taking a break from a dig
he was working on in Mexico. He was holidaying in New
Orleans at the time, and his initial encounter with Jason
took place in the street outside one of the many bars and
taverns. He, Jason, had been rolling drunk at the time,
he remembered wryly, and was losing the fight he was having with the burly bartender when Durham recognised a
fellow Englishman and intervened. He had settled the bill,
which had been the cause of the fight, and the bartender,
recognising the fact that a sober Jason would have little
difficulty in laying him out, had been more than willing to
accept the settlement. Durham had taken Jason to his lodgings, sobered him up, and eventually persuaded him to
admit to his abortive foray into the real estate business.
Subsequently, he had offered him a job working with him in
Mexico, and although Jason had known little about archae-
ology, he had been willing to learn.

He worked with Durham for almost two years before
they discovered the ruins of the Mayan pyramid, and
beneath, untouched for hundreds of years, the burial
chamber. Even now, so many years after, Jason could remember the thrill they had felt upon discovering the neck-
laces and rings and bracelets that decked the crumbling
skeleton the chamber had contained, and the jade mask
that hid the hollow eye-sockets and gaping mouth.

With his share of what was left after the government had
taken their dues, Durham intended to create a research
institute in England, but Jason had decided to spend some
time in South America. He lived in Brazil for a year, and
then twelve years ago he had bought some land in Santa
Vittoria, a tiny country sandwiched between Brazil and
Uruguay. Although he and Durham had intended to keep
in touch, England was a long way from his home at San
Gabriel, and somehow he had never found the time to write
letters. He had had much to learn—about growing maize

and flax, planting orchards of fruit trees, so that he could harvest his own oranges and lemons, peaches and grapes, but mostly about breeding the horses and cattle which were his real love. It was almost as if he had spent his whole life searching for that one reality, and once he found it, he held it fast. And then, six weeks ago, he got the letter . . .

The ringing of the telephone interrupted his train of thought, and moving lithely across the room, he lifted the receiver.

'Tarrant,' he supplied tersely, and then relaxed when the hotel operator said: 'There's a young lady here to see you, Mr Tarrant. She says you're expecting——'

'That's right,' Jason interrupted the flow. 'You can send her right up.'

'Yes, sir.'

'Oh——' Jason chewed on his lower lip for a moment, 'I'm—er—I'm also expecting someone else. A boy. When he arrives, let me know at once, will you?'

'Yes, Mr Tarrant.'

Jason replaced the receiver on its rest thoughtfully, flexing his shoulder muscles as he contemplated the interview ahead. This wasn't quite his line—interviewing a prospective tutor for the boy, particularly a female one, but there seemed few male tutors willing to abandon the bright lights of London for a remote ranch house in the Sierra Grande. He hoped the woman wasn't too young, although these days appearances could be deceptive, and Estelita wouldn't approve of him taking any female under the age of thirty-five into his home.

As he waited he crossed the room again, catching a glimpse of himself in the long Chinese mirrors that flanked the marble fireplace, an anachronism now in the centrally heated hotel. A wry smile crossed his lips at the image of the dark-suited businessman they reflected, his lean frame encased in the mohair jacket, pants and waistcoat which the tailor in Valvedra had assured him was the latest fashion. Certainly his attire gave the illusion of a man

accustomed to city ways, but Jason couldn't wait to don
the mud-coloured shirts and Levis which were his usual
garb back home. Instead of fine suede, he would wear
leather gaucho boots, and his dark hair, so smoothly
combed, would be rough beneath the wide brim of his
slouch hat. His lips twisted as he wondered what Charles
Durham would think if he could see him now. The older
man would no doubt have been proud of his success, and
he regretted the carelessness which had lengthened the
distance between them all these years. Still, it was too late
now to feel remorse. Instead, he would do everything in his
power to give the boy the home he himself had lacked.

He surveyed the luxurious hotel suite with critical eyes.
Was this the most suitable place to conduct an interview of
this kind? he wondered. Ought he to have had another
woman present? But who? He knew few people in London.
The hotel receptionist perhaps. She had certainly shown
sufficient interest in him when he arrived, but without false
modesty he admitted that the kind of interest she had
shown was hardly appropriate to the occasion. No, this was
something he was going to have to do alone, and trust his
own judgment in assessing the woman's capabilities.

He paced a trifle restlessly across to the fireplace. The
two men he had interviewed for the post had both laboured
under the misapprehension that because he was a wealthy
man he must needs live in Puerto Novo or Valvedra. When
they learned that his *estancia* was over a hundred miles
from the coast, they quickly lost interest in working in such
remote surroundings. So why should a woman feel any
differently? His eyes narrowed. Unless she was some dried-
up old spinster, who saw this post as a golden opportunity
to ingratiate herself with the master of the household. He
grimaced. He was cynical, he admitted it. But years of hard
living and fending for himself had taught him never to trust
anyone's motives at face value. Only Charles Durham had
ever helped him, and now he was dead Jason was determined to do what he could for his son—but not at the cost

of his own freedom. He had had one taste of so-called connubial bliss, and like the use of methadone in drug addiction, it had cured him of the craving. He liked women, he couldn't deny it. He was like any normal healthy male in that respect. But marriage no longer figured in his plans —a circumstance that fired Estelita's hot Latin blood.

A knock at the outer door of the suite brought him upright with a certain tightening of his flat stomach muscles. Stretching the long brown fingers at his sides, he strode purposefully across the room and swung open the door. Then he stood back aghast as a smiling girl of perhaps sixteen years of age stepped forward and, reaching up, bestowed a kiss on each of his taut brown cheeks. A little above medium height and slender, she was only slightly boyish in her fringed suede pants suit, the long curtains of silvery fair hair which fell from a centre parting easily decrying such a supposition. Silky gold-tipped lashes framed wide eyes of a smoky shade of violet, while the smiling mouth was full and generous.

'Jason!' she said, and her voice was low and husky. 'Yes, it has to be. You're exactly as Daddy described you.'

'Daddy!'

Jason was feeling distinctly confused now, particularly when the girl passed him to enter the suite uninvited, looking about her with evident fascination.

'Look—who are you?' he exclaimed, but even as he asked the question he knew, and a sinking feeling invaded the lower regions of his abdomen. 'You . . . can't be . . .'

'Alex Durham, yes.' The girl turned, unconsciously graceful in all her movements. 'Weren't you expecting me?'

Jason's mouth opened and closed on an ominously thin scowl. '*Alex* Durham?' he repeated tersely, and her smile gave way to a grimace of uncertainty.

'Alexandra, actually,' she admitted. Then, adopting a defiant stance, she added: 'Everyone calls me Alex.'

'Do they?' Realising the door was still standing open,

Jason closed it, albeit reluctantly, with a definite click. 'But you knew I thought you were a boy, didn't you?'

'Did you?' She lifted her shoulders in an offhand gesture. 'I'm sorry. I didn't think it would make that much difference.'

Jason moved away from the door, annoyed to find that it was he who was disconcerted here. The correspondence he had had with Durham's solicitors had not been explicit. Obviously, in the circumstances, they had assumed that he would know the age and sex of the child. Child? His lips tightened. Even after so short an acquaintance, Jason could see that Alexandra Durham was not a child. How old was she? Charles had never mentioned a wife in all the time he had known him, and consequently Jason had assumed he had married after returning to England. That would make the boy—girl!—twelve at most, whereas this girl was obviously fifteen or sixteen at least. A shorter guardianship than he had expected perhaps, but what a complication!

'Do you live here?' the girl was asking now, and Jason forced himself to concentrate on what she was saying.

'No, of course not,' he retorted, rather snappishly. 'You know my home is in Santa Vittoria.'

'I meant while you were in England,' she explained politely, her reasonableness irritating Jason even more. 'I've never stayed in an hotel. The nuns didn't approve of that sort of thing. Some of the girls used to spend holidays with their parents, you know, at places like St Moritz and Chamonix in the winter, or Nice or St Tropez or Cap d'Antibes in the summer, but I've never been to those places. Daddy was always on some dig or other——'

'Just a minute.' Jason halted this monologue with a curt intervention. 'Don't you think you ought to explain why you chose to leave me in ignorance of the fact that you're female, and what the hell you expect me to do about it as you are?'

She frowned then, a furrow appearing on the smooth brow. 'What I expect you to do about it?' she repeated softly. 'What do you mean? You're my guardian, aren't you? Whatever sex I happen to be.'

Jason expelled his breath on a heavy sigh. 'I can't believe you're that naïve, *Miss* Durham. You know as well as I do that I expected a boy!'

'So you keep telling me, but I don't see what I can do about *that*,' she retorted, half laughingly, and her amusement was the last straw as far as Jason was concerned.

'Then I'll tell you,' he snapped angrily. 'Your father was a good friend to me when I needed one, and I've never forgotten it. When I heard that he'd died leaving his—child—in my care, I was prepared to do everything in my power to give the boy a decent start in life——'

'I know,' she exclaimed, covering the space between them and laying a hand on the sleeve of his mohair jacket, but he brushed her away, continuing:

'My correspondence with you was addressed to *Master* Alex Durham, and you know it. All my arrangements, all my plans, have been for a boy of perhaps twelve, thirteen years of age——'

'Well, I can't help that,' she protested now, the movement of her head spilling the swathe of silky hair across the dark green suede of her jacket. 'I didn't ask to be willed to you. I couldn't choose what sex I was. If I could, believe me I'd have satisfied you in every detail!'

'What do you mean?'

'Only that my father never wanted a daughter, any more than you want me now,' she retorted, and Jason felt a twinge of remorse for the pained anguish in her eyes. 'I'd have been a boy all right. Then perhaps Daddy might have taken me with him on his trips to Greece and South America, instead of leaving me in the convent until I thought I should die of boredom!'

Jason's eyes narrowed. 'Exactly how old are you?'

'Seventeen!'

'Seventeen?' He stared at her disbelievingly. 'But—but——'

'Daddy never mentioned me?' She shrugged, but he could tell she was fighting her emotions. 'That doesn't surprise me. He never wanted to get married, you know. He never should have. Then—then when my mother died when I was born—well . . .' She shrugged again. 'He put me in the care of the nuns at Sainte Sœur.'

Jason shook his head. 'You speak very good English. But the convent was in France, I gather.'

'Yes. Just outside Paris, actually. My mother was French, you see. But many of the nuns at the convent were English, and my father insisted that as he spoke little French, I should be educated in his language.'

'I see.' Jason ran an impatient hand round the back of his neck, trying to restrain the sense of injustice that was threatening to erupt once more. How could Durham have ignored his child's existence to the extent that never once in the two years he had known him had he mentioned the fact that he had a daughter? It was cold and callous; and totally out of keeping with the man he had thought he had known. But perhaps that was exactly why Durham had helped *him*, out of a sense of guilt towards this—girl, this child, who could have been little more than an infant when Durham was excavating at Los Lobos. Then: 'You say— your father mentioned me?'

'Yes!' Animation entered the girl's features again. 'I don't know whether he wrote you about his expeditions, but towards the end, when he was confined . . .' she faltered, '. . . confined to his bed, he spoke about you a lot.'

Jason drew a deep breath and gestured towards one of the low comfortable couches that faced one another across the width of the hearth. 'Look,' he said. 'I think you'd better sit down. We have to talk, and I guess—I guess it would be easier if we at least tried to understand one another.'

'Of course.' The girl's smile reappeared, and she subsided obediently on to cushions of dark blue brocade. As she did so, the lapels of her jacket parted to reveal the dusky hollow between her breasts, and their rounded fullness pressing against the soft suede was an added indication of her burgeoning maturity. Jason hesitated a moment, and then, with some reluctance, took the couch opposite her, stretching his long legs out in front of him, his fingers curving loosely over the cushions on either side of him.

'Now,' he said, when she raised inquisitive eyebrows, 'tell me a little about what happened to your father— after he returned from Mexico.'

'Oh ...' Alexandra frowned. 'Well, that isn't too easy. I didn't always know where he was or what he was doing. I think he financed an expedition to Egypt, but I'm not sure.'

'But the institute,' said Jason patiently. 'What about the research institute?' The girl looked puzzled now, and his own frown returned. 'Your father intended to use the money he gained from our successful excavation at Los Lobos to create a research institute,' he explained, but Alexandra clearly had no knowledge of this.

'I'm sorry,' she said. 'If—if you think my father died a wealthy man——'

'I didn't say that!' retorted Jason shortly, stung by the implication, and she went on:

'Every penny he had went to finance his last expedition. It was to Turkey—a remote valley in the Taurus mountains. That was where he was taken ill, you see. A chill, followed by a lung infection. They'd been living in tents at the dig, and by the time they got him down to the hospital in Maras it had developed into pneumonia. He recovered, of course, but he wasn't strong enough to go on, and he was flown back to London. That was when he sent for me.'

'And how long ago was that?' asked Jason, watching the play of emotions across her expressive features.

'Six months, I guess,' she answered at once. 'Perhaps he realised the lung infection had weakened the muscles of his heart, and that he hadn't long to live. Or maybe he just wanted to get to know his daughter ...' The words trailed away as a trace of emotion brought a slightly higher note to her voice, but she controlled it. 'I didn't know he'd written to the solicitor—until after—after he was dead. He knew I wouldn't have wanted him to. I mean—I'm quite capable of taking care of myself, you know.'

'Are you?' Jason's tone was dry, but inwardly he admired her spirit. It could not have been an easy six months, whatever way you looked at it.

'Yes.' She squared her shoulders now and looked at him. 'Well? Are you going to disown me?'

'No!' Jason's denial was abrupt, and pushing himself up with his hands, he stood over her, tall and dark and slightly menacing, although he was unaware of it. 'I just need some time to—to revise my plans.'

She rose too, then, and the scent of some perfume she was wearing rose disturbingly to his nostrils. It was fresh and slightly heady, like the lemon groves back home, and for a moment he looked down at her, his dark eyes mirroring the gentler shade of hers. Unwillingly, his senses stirred at the unconscious allure of those gold-fringed irises, pansy-soft as she gazed up at him.

'Thank you,' she said, and quite unselfconsciously pressed two fingers against her lips before transferring them to his mouth. 'Daddy was right about you. You are a good man.'

What Jason would have replied to this totally unexpected provocation he hardly knew, but a sudden knocking at the door to the suite provided a welcome distraction. Of course, he thought abstractedly, it would be the governess, the woman he had been waiting to interview when this frustrating creature erupted into his life. At least the interruption would give him a breathing space, he thought savagely, furious with himself for allowing a girl—little more than a schoolgirl—to disrupt his normally controlled emotions.

'This is going to be awkward,' he said, putting some space between them as he spoke. 'I imagine this is the woman I intended interviewing for the post of—of governess.'

'Governess!' Alexandra echoed, the violet eyes dancing now. 'For me?' She gurgled with laughter. 'Oh, Jason, did you really think I would need a governess?'

Jason's thinning mouth sobered her however. 'It may surprise you to know that as your father never mentioned your existence, I assumed he had married since our expedition to Los Lobos. Naturally, therefore, I expected a younger child.'

'I'm not a child,' she pointed out, unable to let that go, but he had already turned away to open the door.

The woman who was waiting outside was reassuringly middle-aged. Jason guessed her age to be somewhere between forty-five and fifty, and her dress and appearance were in keeping with her profession. If only she had arrived first, he found himself thinking impatiently. Then perhaps he would have been more prepared to deal with his unexpectedly female ward.

'Mr Tarrant?' the woman was asking politely, and Jason nodded shortly, offering his hand in greeting and gesturing for the woman to come in.

'You are Miss Holland, I take it?' he enquired brusquely, and that lady agreed with his admission.

'I'm sorry I'm late,' she apologised, as he closed the door behind them, and her eyes alighted questioningly on Alexandra. 'I—er—I couldn't get a cab, and then the traffic . . .'

'That's quite all right, Miss Holland,' Jason assured her curtly, his eyes flickering briefly over the slender figure by the hearth. 'As it happens, your being late has precipitated a situation which I'm afraid alters matters considerably.'

'Oh?' Miss Holland's glance lingered once more on Alexandra's slim youthfulness, and a rather worried look crossed her homely features. It occurred to Jason that perhaps getting the job had meant a lot to this rather anxious-looking woman, and his deepening interest observed the faintly worn sleeves of her navy-blue uniform coat, and the neat but unmistakable darns in her woollen gloves.

Now he offered her a chair and after she was seated, he explained: 'I'm afraid the post I advertised no longer exists. The—er—the boy turns out to be a girl, and she——' he turned abruptly and indicated Alexandra, 'as you can see, is too old to require a governess.'

Miss Holland's worn features mirrored her disappointment. 'Yes,' she said. 'Yes, I see.'

'I'm sorry . . .' And he was. Jason cast another impatient glance in Alexandra's direction. Why couldn't she have been the child he expected? Why hadn't Durham told him the truth? He knew instinctively that Miss Holland would have taken the post, wherever it was. She had that sort of defeated air about her that smacked of too many interviews and too many disappointments. Nowadays, people wanted modern young governessess for their children, not middle-aged women, however well qualified. Miss Holland just wanted to work, and he wondered how long it was since she had done so. Still, he reflected wryly, he had enough problems of his own right now. He couldn't be blamed for what was indisputably evident.

The woman rose to her feet again now and faced him with a touching air of confidence. 'I'll be going then, Mr Tarrant. Thank you for seeing me. And I'm sorry things haven't worked out as—as you expected.' Faint colour ran up her cheeks as she realised what she was implying, and she added hastily: 'I mean, of course, *I'm* sorry. You—er—you may not be. I'm sure you're not. That is——'

'That's quite all right, Miss Holland,' Jason intervened smoothly, halting her embarrassed flow, and smiling to remove any sharpness from his words. 'I know exactly what you mean.'

Miss Holland nodded, compressed her lips, offered a half smile of apology to Alexandra, and moved towards the door. Jason strode ahead of her, swinging open the door as she approached, and taking the hand she tentatively offered him in farewell.

'Good luck,' he said, as she pulled on her shabby glove, and her smile was more eloquent than any words.

With the door closed behind her, Jason leant against it almost wearily. What now? What was he going to do with the girl? One thing was certain, he could not take her back to San Gabriel with him. Apart from Estelita, his was a masculine household, and there was no place in it for a provocative teenager just waiting to try her claws. Besides, there was nothing for a girl at his *estancia*. The life he led was almost spartan in its simplicity, and remote from any kind of social gathering. With a boy, it would have been different. He could have shown him the ranch, taught him to ride and rope a steer, taught him to break horses and sleep out under the stars when the yearly round-up was made; treated him like a son, in fact, the son he was never likely to have now. But a girl . . . In God's name, what could he do for her?

As if aware of the turmoil inside him, Alexandra left her place by the hearth to approach him, and he stiffened as she halted some few feet away from him.

'What's the matter?' she asked, and her eyes were guarded now. 'What are you thinking? Do you want to change your mind about me?'

'Change my mind?' Jason frowned. 'I don't know what you mean.'

Alexandra's long lashes swept her cheeks. 'I think you do. You're wishing I was a boy, too, aren't you? Just like Daddy.' Her chin lifted, and her eyes were defiant as they sought his. 'What is it with you two? What's wrong with being a woman? Don't they have their uses, too?'

Jason straightened away from the door. 'All right,' he admitted abruptly. 'I don't deny it. I was thinking along those lines. But only because your being a girl makes everything that much more complicated.'

'Why?'

'Why?' A faintly mocking gleam invaded his eyes. 'Oh, come on, Miss Durham, I don't believe you're that unsophisticated.'

'Will you please stop calling me *Miss* Durham! My name's Alex—Alexandra, if you like, or perhaps not, as you seem to prefer the masculine gender!'

Jason's mouth tightened at the deliberately insolent intonation, but he let it go, saying quietly: 'I was merely going to explain that had you been a boy, you could have accompanied me back to Santa Vittoria, and made your home with me at San Gabriel.'

'San Gabriel?' For a moment, she was diverted. 'What's that? Your house?'

'My ranch, yes.'

'How super!' Her eyes sparkled. 'Oh, yes, Jason, I'd like to do that.'

'Now wait a minute . . .' Jason was finding it increasingly difficult to control this conversation. 'I said—had you been a boy——'

'But what does it matter?' she exclaimed. 'So long as I want to go?'

'So long as *you* want to go!' Jason raised his eyes heavenward for a moment in a gesture of frustration. 'My dear Miss—*Alexandra*! You know perfectly well I can't take you to San Gabriel.'

Her dark brows arched. 'Your wife would object?'

'I don't have a wife.'

'Ah, no . . .' She rubbed her nose thoughtfully with her finger. 'You wouldn't.'

'What the hell do you mean?'

Jason spoke angrily, and her lips twitched. 'Why, nothing. Only that—you're a misogynist, aren't you?'

'No, damn you, I'm not!' Jason found he was unaccountably furious. 'I enjoy a *woman*'s company as well as the next man. I just don't intend taking a promiscuous schoolgirl back to a ranch where the men don't see a white woman from one year's end to the next!'

A gurgle of laughter escaped her at this. 'Make up your mind,' she taunted him. 'Either I'm a schoolgirl or a woman —which?'

'You know what I mean,' he grated severely. 'Now, I suggest we discuss what it is you want to do with your life.'

'I want to stay with you. Either here or at San Gabriel.' She sighed. 'Hmm, that's a beautiful name, isn't it? Is the ranch as beautiful as its name? Or is it an *estancia*? Isn't that what they call ranches in South America?'

'*Alexandra!*'

The warning note in his voice went unheeded as she smiled impishly up at him. 'That's better,' she approved. 'I like the way you say my name. What sort of accent would you say you have? I think it's a sort of mid-Atlantic accent, isn't it? Neither one thing nor the other.'

Jason turned from her to pace tensely towards the window. This was hopeless. He was getting absolutely no-where. He half wished he had asked Miss Holland to remain during the course of this interview. Maybe she would have been able to make some constructive suggestion, explain to the girl that what she was asking was impossible. *God*, why had Charles done this to him? Surely he must have known the complications it would bring. What had been his intention? What had he expected Jason to do with her? Surely he could not have wanted him to take her back with him to South America. Hadn't he cared about the dangers the obvious temptation a girl like her would present to men starved of the company of women? And what of his erstwhile colleague? What had he really known of him, that he should feel able to entrust his daughter to his care?

'Jason . . .' Alexandra's husky voice right behind him made him aware she had moved to join him by the window. 'Jason, please—can't we talk about this? I know I must have been a great shock to you, and I admit, I did leave you in ignorance deliberately, but only because—well, be-cause I was afraid you might—you might not come . . .'

'And what kind of a swine would I have been if I hadn't?'
Jason demanded, glancing at her broodingly. 'My God,
whatever his reasons, your father has left you in my care, at
least until you're eighteen, and I should not have shirked
that responsibility.'

'Oh, *responsibility* . . .' She scuffed her toe against the
expensive rug with ill grace. 'I don't want to be a *responsibility*! I'm a person, a human being; a living entity in my
own right. I don't want to be anyone's responsibility. I just
want to be—to be a part of your life, part of someone's life
anyway,' she finished a trifle wistfully.

Jason's teeth grated. 'You won't try and understand, will
you?'

'What's to understand?' She held his gaze deliberately.
'Are you afraid of me, *Mr* Tarrant? Are you afraid you
might be as—tempted as the next man——'

'Don't be so ridiculous!' Jason's rejection of her taunting
statement was violent, but she stood her ground. 'I'm
simply trying to explain to you that my *gauchos* are not
the fanciful gallants you've probably seen on the screen.
They're rough men, mestizos and Indians for the most part,
for whom an unattached white girl is fair game. Do I make
myself clear?'

'Perfectly,' she conceded, without flinching. 'But surely
as your—ward, I would merit some respect.'

'Perhaps. But I don't feel like being nursemaid!'

'And that's the truth, isn't it?' she declared bitterly. 'Oh,
you're just like my father!'

She presented her back to him then, groping in the bag
that hung from one shoulder for the handkerchief she
couldn't find. Jason watched her helpless fumblings for
several minutes, and then extracted his own handkerchief
from his pocket and handed it to her.

But instead of thanking him, as he had expected, she
snatched the pristine square of white linen and threw it on
the floor, deliberately grinding the heel of her boot upon
it. Jason stared, bleak-eyed, as she kicked the now soiled

handkerchief aside, and rubbed her nose unhygienically on the back of her hand.

'Why, you——'

'Go on!' she encouraged him, chancing a look at him over her shoulder. 'Say it! Call me names. Better that than ignoring my existence!'

Jason allowed his breath to escape on a suppressed oath, then bent and lifted the grubby handkerchief. He regarded it solemnly for several seconds, then he stuffed it back into the pocket of his jacket. Alexandra was sniffing now, her head bent, but he made no attempt to comfort her. Instead, he drew a case of the long narrow cigars he liked from his pocket, and placing one between his teeth, applied the flame of his lighter to it.

The aromatic flavour was soothing, and he attempted to remain calm. Arguing with the girl was doing no good, he could see that. But somehow he had to make her see reason. A sudden idea occurred to him. What she needed was someone to take care of her, some woman, and almost instantaneously the image of Miss Holland sprang to his mind. If that lady could be persuaded to accept a position as housekeeper-cum-guardian, he could lease a house here in London, and Alexandra could choose whether she wanted to continue with her studies or alternatively find some suitable occupation. He might even permit her to visit him in Santa Vittoria on occasion. If she stayed at the hotel in Valvedra, there was no reason why she shouldn't travel if she wanted to.

'Alexandra . . .' His own voice was almost persuasive now, and instinctively she responded to the gentler tone.

'Yes?' She half turned, and he glimpsed the tear-washed brilliance of her eyes, tiny globules glistening like raindrops on her lashes. Unaccountably, he was stirred, and the knowledge brought an impatient hardening in his voice.

'I've come to a decision,' he said, thrusting his balled fists into the pockets of his pants, unaware that the action drew her attention to the powerful muscles of his thighs.

'I shall lease a house here in London, for you—and for Miss Holland——'

'Miss Holland?'

'That's right. The woman who was here a few minutes ago. If I'm not mistaken, she needs a job badly. Maybe she will be prepared to act as your guardian in my absence——'

'No!'

'What do you mean—*no*?' he demanded ominously. 'Alexandra, might I remind you that until your eighteenth birthday, I *am* your guardian. You will do as I say.'

'You can't make me,' she retorted, swinging round to face him. 'Oh, I admit, while you're here, you can force me to stay with Miss—Miss Holland, but after you're gone, do you honestly believe she'll be able to make me do as she says? She can't lock me in my room, you know. I shall have to go out sometimes. And who says I'll have to come back?'

His face was steely hard by the time she had finished. 'Are you threatening me?' he demanded, and she sensed the tautening of his body.

'I—why, no. Not—threatening,' she muttered, resorting to looking for her handkerchief again. 'But . . .' She caught her lower lip between her teeth and looked up at him again, and this time there was only appeal in those drowned violet depths. 'Oh, Jason, *please*! Don't do this. Let me come with you. I'll be good, I promise. I won't go near any of your farmhands—*gauchos*, whatever. I'll do exactly as *you* say. I can cook—and clean—and make beds——'

'No, Alexandra!'

'Why not? Why not?' Instead of spitting at him again as he had half expected, she closed the gap between them and he tore his hands out of his pockets to prevent her from getting too close for comfort. 'Jason, Daddy respected you so much. He wanted us to be friends. Won't you at least try to like me?'

Jason's hands had descended on her shoulders, and the fragile vulnerability of the bones beneath his fingers caused him to hesitate before saying, 'It's not a question of—*liking*, Alexandra.'

'Then why——'

He found he was not immune to those eyes after all. Hurting her was like hurting a wounded deer, a trite observation, but true nevertheless. What the hell, her father had abandoned her, hadn't he? Was he about to do the same? What would happen to her if he did? Who knew what dangers she might encounter in London, particularly in her desire to prove to him that she needed his protection? His fingers tightened so that he felt the bones might crack beneath his hold, but she didn't wince, and with a feeling compounded of sympathy and compassion, and a curious kind of self-disgust, he said:

'All right, all right, I give in. You can come with me to Santa Vittoria. You and Miss Holland both.'

'You really mean it?'

Tears overspilled her eyes as she stared disbelievingly up at him, and almost with revulsion he thrust her away from him. But that didn't alter the fact that by allowing her to accompany him, he sensed he was inviting trouble. What form that trouble would take, he could not foresee, but almost immediately he wished he could retract his words.

It was too late, of course. Much too late. The misty relief that shone in her eyes could not be doused, and far from regretting his submission, she was positively incoherent with delight.

'Oh, Jason!' she breathed, brushing away her tears with a careless hand, and before he could anticipate what she was about to do, she had flung her arms around his neck and was bestowing kisses all over his face. 'Darling, darling Jason!' she was crying exuberantly, while he tried rather unsuccessfully to free himself, uncomfortably aware of those firm breasts pressing against the material of his waistcoat and of the warm scent of her arms wound so closely round his neck. If she was to accompany him to

San Gabriel, they would have to talk about her impulsive methods of expressing herself, he thought dryly. He wondered how she saw him. As some kind of Dutch uncle, perhaps, or the father figure she had never known. Whatever, she would have to learn that young women, however enthusiastic, did not throw themselves into the arms of a virtual stranger just because he had agreed to her wishes, albeit against his better judgment.

Having extracted himself, and with her wrists pressed firmly against her sides, Jason felt more able to speak seriously to her, although the dancing violet eyes were a continual distraction.

'Miss Holland,' he said, 'Miss Holland must agree to come with us, do you understand? If she refuses——'

'She won't,' Alexandra interrupted certainly. 'She liked you, I'm sure.'

'It's you she has to deal with,' retorted Jason repressively, wondering with some misgivings how Estelita would react to two such females in his house. 'And while we're on the subject, you must not be so—so demonstrative.'

'Demonstrative?' Alexandra's brows arched. 'Towards you, you mean?'

'Towards anyone,' amended Jason dryly, but she only smiled.

'Why?' she persisted. 'Don't you like it? Don't you like me to touch you?'

'That has nothing to do with it,' he began, but she shook her head.

'I think it has.' She tried to free her wrists, but he knew better than to let her go. 'I think it has everything to do with it. At the convent—you know, when I was living with the nuns—nobody ever touched one another. We were like—separate species.' She sighed. 'We used to talk together—and smile together—even pray together. But we never touched.' She moved her slim shoulders in a helpless gesture. 'I think people should touch one another. That's what caring is all about.' She lifted her head. 'I like touching people. I like touching you . . .'

'That's enough!'

Abruptly, she was free, but she knew better than to touch him just then. After a moment's laboured breathing, he turned and crossed to the telephone, and while she watched, he asked the operator to get him the number of the agency where he had engaged to interview the governess. It was a brief call, but it served a dual purpose—on the one hand, it accomplished the need to contact Miss Holland as quickly as possible, and on the other it gave him time to realise the enormity of the task he was taking upon himself.

CHAPTER TWO

ALEXANDRA had never experienced such a sense of space and freedom, miles and miles of long pampas grass stretching as far as the eye could see. Acres and acres of land, grazed by herds of shorthorn cattle, that turned wicked eyes in their direction as they passed, making Alexandra, at least, aware of the thin sheet of metal which separated them from those ugly pointed projections. Cattle in France and England never had such beady little eyes, or moved with the arrogance of the beast, untamed and magnificent.

Ever since the powerful Range-Rover passed beneath the crossed strips of wood which had marked the boundary of Jason's land, she had been expecting to see the ranch-house, but mile followed mile and there was nothing in sight but the untrammelled grasslands of the Santa Vittorian plateau. The road, which from Valvedra had been passably smooth, was now little more than a beaten track, and she was regretting her impulse to offer Miss Holland the seat beside Jason in front. As she sat in the back of the Range-Rover, the base of her spine was in constant opposition to the springs of the vehicle, and her back ached from being thrown from side to side.

From time to time, her eyes encountered Jason's through the rear-view mirror, and then she made a determined effort to appear unconcerned, aware that occasionally a trace of amusement lightened their umber depths. But she was here, that was the main thing, she thought with satisfaction, and the awareness of Jason's lean body in the seat in front of her was all the compensation she needed.

It had not been easy, she acknowledged it now, and until the moment she and Miss Holland had boarded the plane she had been terrified in case he should send some message

forbidding her to join him. But from the minute her father
had spoken of Jason Tarrant, describing the kind of man
he was, telling her about their adventures in Mexico, the
rough absorbing outdoor life they had led, she had wanted
to meet him. All her life she had wanted to do the things
her father did, meet the people he worked with, and share
in the thrill of his excavations. She would have followed
him to the ends of the earth if he had asked her, but he
never had. So far as he was concerned, she was a girl, and
girls were not welcome in what he considered to be a male
province. Her own mother had died in childbirth confirming
his belief that females were weak, defenceless creatures,
and he had only sent for Alexandra at the end because he
had known he was dying, too.

Even then, he had not known what to do with her. Her
assurances that she would make out on her own had not
convinced him, but his suggestion of returning her to the
nuns of Sainte Sœur had filled her with alarm. It was then
she had coined the idea of writing to Jason Tarrant, of telling him her father was dying, and putting her future into
his hands. She knew her father had helped him when he
was in trouble, but Charles Durham would not even consider such a proposition. Instead, he had dictated a letter
to his solicitors, giving them the address of the convent,
and asking that if—*when*—anything happened to him,
Alexandra should return there, at least until she was
eighteen.

To her shame, Alexandra had never written that letter.
Because his eyesight was failing, she had written all her
father's letters for him, and it wasn't difficult to substitute
a letter of her own for him to sign. It was possible that
given time, the solicitors might have questioned that
particular missive, but Charles Durham suffered a massive
heart attack the following day from which he never recovered. Alexandra was left, pale and distraught, at the
mercy of her own machinations.

Her first meeting with Jason, at his hotel, had not been

exactly as she had expected. Of course, she had expected him to protest about the fact of her being a girl—*didn't everyone?*—but she had not imagined he would be so young. She had been prepared to meet a contemporary of her father's, a man in his fifties, at least, instead of someone perhaps twenty years younger. But that initial hazard had been swiftly superseded by her immediate attraction to the man himself, whose lean hard body and dark-skinned features reminded her vividly of the painting of an Indian the nuns had kept at the convent. Those gentle women would have been shocked by Alexandra's reactions to that particular picture, the baptism to Christianity of a tall bronzed pagan, which had taken on a different aspect in Alexandra's maturing eyes.

Jason himself had been as confounded as her father by his new responsibilities, but in the event it proved providential that he had imagined her to be a boy. Without Miss Holland's intervention, he might never have been persuaded to allow her to go to Santa Vittoria, but she felt now that whatever he had decreed, she would have followed him. It was fate, she decided, which had prompted her to write that letter, and for now, just being with him was enough.

Miss Holland was another matter. That lady had taken her responsibilities very seriously, and seemed to regard her situation as that of a nursemaid, rather than a companion. There were times when she made Alexandra feel like a child in the company of an adult, and those occasions were galling. She was seventeen; granted she had led a comparatively sheltered life, but she had read a lot, much of it books the nuns would have been horrified to discover in the hands of one of their charges. The only thing her father had not kept her short of was money and she had spent it lavishly on literature of all kinds. All her experience of the relationship between a man and a woman had come from books, but she felt adequate to cope should the situation arise. She was a mature and intelligent young woman, or so she believed, and Miss Holland's behaviour was a source of irritation to her. The fact that since their arrival in Valvedra, it was a source of amusement to Jason, too, only added to her frustration.

Miss Holland had proved useful when it came to providing her with a wardrobe suitable to the climate in which she was to be living. Her knowledge of London was extensive, she having tutored the children of a titled family for more years than she cared to admit, and maybe because she regarded Alexandra as little more than a child, she chose those shops where teenage clothes were sold. Once inside those shops however, Alexandra soon made her own wishes felt, and the sales assistants added their encouragement. The fashions of the day—jeans and sweaters, pants suits, and long flowing skirts and dresses—looked good on Alexandra's slender figure, and although Miss Holland looked askance at revealing smocks and skin-tight jumpers, her opinion was overruled. Besides, the ear-splitting music which was an accompaniment to the service in these establishments gave her a headache, and she was obliged to wait outside.

Although Charles Durham had not died a poor man, he had not died a rich one either. He had used most of his capital to finance the expeditions which had become the cornerstone of his life, and sacrificed his dream of creating an institute in the tireless search for knowledge. Even so, the sale of the small house he had owned, though seldom occupied, in Ealing did provide Alexandra with a comfortable nest-egg, but her plans of bestowing it on her benefactor were doomed to disappointment. Before departing for South America, Jason had made it very clear that until her majority, he intended to make himself responsible for her maintenance, and the knowledge that she had tricked him into supporting her occasionally gave her a sleepless night. She consoled herself with the belief, however, that once she was living in his house, she would make herself useful to him in every way possible, and somehow she would repay him.

The days following Jason's departure had dragged. She and the middle-aged lady who was to accompany her were obliged to have shots for various tropical diseases before their departure, and because Jason could not spare the time away from his *estancia*, he had left within a week of their first meeting. From then on, Alexandra had lived in a fever of anxiety, as much from the knowledge of her own duplicity as from the after-effects of the vaccination serum.

But eventually the day of departure had arrived, and they had left a cold, grey England, recovering from the chills of January, to fly south into the sun. Their overnight stay in Rio de Janeiro had given Alexandra no thrill, although Miss Holland had marvelled at the twin peaks overlooking Guanabara Bay, and the magnificent statue of Christ whose shadow embraced the city. The thrill for Alexandra had come when they landed the next morning at Valvedra's much smaller airport, and found Jason awaiting them in the arrivals lounge. In mud-coloured Levis and a matching shirt, half open down the muscled darkness of his chest, he appeared relaxed and casual, only the guarded narrowing of his eyes revealing the doubts he still possessed about bringing her here. But Alexandra had determinedly ignored his restraint, and much to both his, and Miss Holland's, disapproval she had flung her arms about his neck and greeted him in her usual impulsive fashion. This time, however, Jason had quickly disengaged himself, and the kiss meant for his mouth had slid harmlessly along his jawline. Alexandra had been sad, but unrepentant, despite the effort of Miss Holland to behave as if she was some kind of annoying child who refused to behave with decorum.

Beyond the windows of the Range-Rover, the ground was steadily rising, and she saw to her surprise that they were in rolling hill country now, granite-like ridges casting shadows across the land. In the distance, the purple peaks of the Sierra Grande looked rugged and mysterious, and the whole aspect of the country had changed. It was late afternoon and already the shadows were lengthening, elongating the branches of the wind-torn cypresses that clung to the ridges, and shedding a rippling wave of ghost-like fingers across the land.

Their emergence into a sunlit valley was almost startling, the escarpment dropping away below them where a stream tumbled recklessly down the cliff face. It was then that Alexandra saw him, outlined against the golden rays of the sinking sun on the ridge opposite them, a magnificent black stallion silhouetted by the purplish gold backdrop of earth and sky. Just for a second he was there and then he was gone, plunging into the gully behind him, so that she thought for a moment she had imagined him.

'Oh!' she gasped, the sound escaping from her on a soft sigh, and Jason's response was one of wry satisfaction.

'You saw him.' It was a statement, not a question, and Miss Holland, unaware of the tableau, gave an exclamation of surprise.

'I beg your par——' she was beginning, when Alexandra leant forward to rest her arms along the backs of their seats, saying eagerly: 'Yes. Yes, I saw him! Whose is he? Is he yours? Oh, Jason, he's beautiful!'

Jason gave her a half mocking glance over his shoulder. 'I doubt that brute will ever belong to anybody,' he remarked flatly. 'I suppose technically, yes, you could say that as he runs on my land, he belongs to me, but no one's ever succeeded in breaking him.'

'You have caught him, then?'

'Yes.' Jason nodded, and Miss Holland's expression grew even more confused. 'But he's a proud bastard—excuse me!' This as that lady's brows ascended. 'He considers running my range with my mares and keeping them happy his prime objective!'

Alexandra's low laugh was intimate, and as if realising her bare arm was resting comfortably against the broad expanse of his shoulder, Jason's expression hardened and he moved so that she was not touching him. Fortunately, perhaps, Miss Holland chose that moment to ask a question of her own, and Alexandra sank back against the upholstery as Jason explained what they had seen.

'You breed horses, Mr. Tarrant?' she enquired, her lips twitching a little as if at a rather distasteful subject, and Jason's hard features softened a little.

'Horses are my passion,' he admitted, his eyes meeting Alexandra's for a brief compelling moment. Then, braking as the road took a sharp curve, he added: 'But the production of beef is my primary concern.'

'But this animal—the one Alexandra has just seen—is a wild creature?' Miss Holland persisted.

'I suppose he is,' Jason nodded, frowning as the wheels of the Range-Rover slid across a shingly patch of pebbles dangerously close to the edge of the track. 'But sometimes I wonder if he's not more civilised than we are.' His lips twisted at the older woman's apparent astonishment. 'There's little that goes on at the *estancia* that he doesn't know about. Some of the Indians think he's the reincarnation of one of their gods. To them, he's sacred. To me, he has less saintly qualities.'

Miss Holland shook her head, obviously disturbed by her first introduction to life at San Gabriel, but Alexandra was filled with a mixture of anticipation and excitement. This was what she had always wanted, she thought with satisfaction; travel and adventure, and a chance to live her life instead of just existing. Jason's disapproval did not disturb her, it was a challenge, and something told her he was not as indifferent to her femininity as he pretended to be.

Then her breath caught in her throat as she suddenly glimpsed a building ahead of them. As yet, it was below them in the valley, but the painted tiles of its roof, leaved across a wide verandah, gave her her first sight of Jason's *hacienda*.

Uncaring of his hostility, Alexandra leant forward again, deliberately allowing her slim fingers to stroke the nape of his neck, hidden beneath the over-long straightness of his hair. 'Is that your house?' she breathed, and the scent of her breath mingled with the perfume of wild verbena that drifted irresistibly through the open windows of the Range-Rover.

Jason's hand came up, ostensibly to smooth his hair, but he pushed her fingers determinedly away, as he answered: 'Yes, that's San Gabriel,' and her delight in her surroundings obliterated the coldness of his tones.

'It's rather a large house, isn't it, Mr Tarrant?'

Miss Holland had her own opinion, and Jason chose to tell her that the sprawling outbuildings she could see were the lodgings of the *gauchos* who worked for him. He pointed out the long bunkhouse and the cookhouse where their meals were served.

'I have twenty men who work for me on a permanent basis, and at least twice that number who are employed if and when we need them. Then there's Ricardo Goya, and Andrés Alberoni, who has his own home at the other end of the valley. Ricardo is my foreman, and Andrés is the best herdsman this side of the Andes.'

'Quite a large establishment.' Miss Holland was impressed, although Alexandra guessed she still had misgivings about coming out here. It could only be all too different from what she was used to, and unlike Alexandra she was old to change her ways. But pride, and necessity, had taken the choice of working conditions out of her hands, and she had been prepared to sacrifice her desire to remain in England for the very adequate salary Jason had offered her.

The road widened as they reached the grassy lower slopes of the valley, and now they could see the river that meandered beside banks bright with golden rod and curiously yellow poppies. There were cows grazing beside the river, not the wild-eyed beasts they had seen on their journey, but fat, placid-looking creatures that were more interested in cropping the grass than watching their passage. As they neared the homestead, Alexandra saw the corrals where they kept the mares and their foals, and nearer at hand, shaggy-haired goats and chickens that scuttled out of their path.

But the *hacienda* itself riveted her gaze. Now, she could see that the low-hanging tiles were a deep red in colour, shading a balcony above the verandah, where rattan chairs suggested a shady retreat on hot afternoons. Right now, with the sun sinking lower every minute, the air was comparatively cool, unlike earlier in the day when Alexandra had had to discard the jerkin that matched her blue cotton pants. Beyond the verandah, she could see a shadowy hallway, framed by the sprawling cluster of vines and honeysuckle which had made their home around the pillars that supported the balcony. At the side of the building, a wrought-iron staircase wound, Spanish-fashion, to the upper floor, and along the balcony Alexandra could see long curtains moving in the breeze from open shutters. The shutters were all folded back at present, green slats against a pale-washed wall, as distinctive in their way as the riot of exotic blossoms that tumbled carelessly from urns beside the verandah steps.

Unable to suppress her delight, Alexandra bounced forward again, but Jason was already stopping the vehicle, and as he began to open his door a woman appeared round the corner of the building. She was young, that much Alexandra registered at a glance, tall, with full swelling breasts, and hair as dark as Jason's own. It was long, like Alexandra's, but whereas hers was inclined to curl in the heat, this woman's was perfectly straight, and fell smoothly over one shoulder. Her features were those of the Madonna, calm and impassive, but as Alexandra alighted from the vehicle, too, she felt a wave of hostility emanating from her that had none of the Virgin's compassion about it.

Jason greeted the woman with a faintly wry expression,

turning first to help his other passenger to climb down, before saying: 'This is my housekeeper, Miss Holland. Señora Vargas. Estelita, this is my ward—and her companion.'

'Hello.'

Alexandra stepped forward, holding out her hand, determined not to be daunted by this sloe-eyed female. Close at hand, she was not half as young as she had at first imagined, but she was not mistaken that the faintly contemptuous stare Estelita conferred upon her sleeveless vest and creased cotton pants was intended to intimidate. The woman's attire of long black skirt and loose-fitting blouse was common to women she had seen in Valvedra, but Estelita bestowed a certain grace upon them which was not typical.

Now, she allowed Alexandra to take her limp hand before saying: '*Bienvenida, señorita!*' in tones which said just the opposite.

'*Inglés*, Estelita,' Jason warned in an undertone, and the housekeeper greeted Miss Holland in her own language, showing more enthusiasm towards the older woman than she had done to the younger one.

'Come inside . . .' Jason was already mounting the steps, and Alexandra quickly followed him meeting his gaze deliberately as he looked back at them. But he refused to answer the question in hers, and strode ahead into the cool, tiled hall of the *hacienda*.

The walls were plain and adorned with small plaques of saints. There were flowers in a copper bowl, huge lilies with thick creamy petals, and orchids, fragile and exotic. There were jewel-bright rugs and a hand-carved chest, and wind-chimes that whispered in the draught of their passing. No one would have taken it for the home of an Englishman, and yet Alexandra felt a sense of homecoming she had never experienced before.

Gazing at the circular window above the gallery of the first floor landing, whose prismatic light slanted down to the hall below, she hardly realised Jason had left her, or that Miss Holland and the woman, Estelita, had come to join her. Until the housekeeper spoke.

'You would like to see your rooms?' she suggested politely. 'I will show them to you while Pepe prepares some tea.' She addressed herself to Miss Holland. 'You would like some tea, *señora*, I am sure.'

'Tea!'

Miss Holland made an obeisance of the word, but Alexandra suddenly realised that Jason was not with them, and looked about her in faint annoyance. Several doors opened from the wide hallway, and through open doors she could see an inner courtyard, but she had no way of knowing where he had gone. Estelita, taking her silence for acquiescence, was already beginning to mount the wrought iron staircase that circled the hall, and Miss Holland was eagerly following.

It was irritating to have to go with them. Alexandra wasn't tired. On the contrary, she was exhilarated, and all too eager to explore her new domain. Jason! she thought impatiently. He must have known how she would feel, and yet he had left her to Estelita's less than friendly overtures.

Her room temporarily overcame her annoyance. Large, and high-ceilinged, it overlooked the whole sweep of the valley, and although the furnishings were not luxurious, their very spareness was attractive. Long woven beige curtains matched the woven bedspread, and the dressing table and long clothes closet left plenty of room for the velvet-cushioned *prie-dieu* in the corner. Two candles could be lighted on either side of the carved wooden cross, and Alexandra was enchanted to discover that the candles were hand-made, too. Miss Holland's room was next door, very little different from that of her charge, and Estelita explained that there was only one bathroom, unfortunately.

'The men use the showers down at the bunkhouse,' she said, when Miss Holland revealed her dismay, and Alexandra asked who she meant.

'Why—Jason, *sin duda*,' she explained with a slight curl to her lip, 'and Ricardo.'

'Ricardo?' Alexandra frowned, noticing the familiar way Estelita spoke of her employer. 'That would be—Mr Tarrant's foreman?'

'That is correct.' Estelita's black eyes were insolent. 'You will meet him at supper, no doubt. Now ...' She turned once more to Miss Holland. 'If you will excuse me, I will see about your tea.'

'Of course, of course.'

Miss Holland was only too willing to agree, but she followed Alexandra into her room when the woman had gone, and sank down rather wearily onto the bed.

'Do you think you're going to be happy here?' she asked, as the girl walked rather thoughtfully towards the open balcony doors, and Alexandra looked back at her with some misgivings.

'Why do you ask that?' she exclaimed, trying to subdue the irritating feeling of anti-climax she herself was feeling, and her companion gave a somewhat helpless shrug of her shoulders.

'I get the feeling we're not altogether welcome,' she confessed, taking out her handkerchief and wiping the grime of the journey from her rather anxious features. 'Oh, not from Mr Tarrant, of course. He's been charming. But Señora Vargas ...'

'*Estelita*,' said Alexandra firmly, more firmly than she was actually feeling, 'Estelita is the housekeeper, that's all. I don't intend to let a housekeeper intimidate me!'

'Do you think that's all she is?' asked Miss Holland doubtfully, unexpectedly voicing those fears which Alexandra had succeeded in keeping hidden until that moment. 'She seems—very much in command to me.'

Alexandra determinedly squared her shoulders. 'Well, maybe she is, at that. But she's not in command of us, Miss Holland, and that's what matters.'

The older woman gave a rueful smile. 'Oh, for the

arrogance of youth!' she murmured, a trifle anxiously, and then started when a male voice spoke brusquely behind them.

'Is everything all right?'

It was Jason, and Alexandra turned to him mutinously, wondering how much of their conversation he had overheard. 'Must you creep up on us like that?' she snapped, thrusting back the weight of her hair with a nervous hand, aware that it must be uncombed and unruly after the journey, and his mouth took a downward curve.

'I did not creep up on you!' he declared coldly. 'I was merely attempting to assure myself that you had everything you needed.'

'Well, we haven't!' said Alexandra childishly, facing him in defiance of her emotions. 'We're short on a host, for one thing, and for another—where did you disappear to?'

Jason's mouth relaxed a little. 'I'm sorry, but I'm afraid this is not a holiday hotel. It's a working ranch, with any number of things waiting to be done. I'm sorry if you think I neglect my duties——'

'Oh, I'm sure we didn't think any such thing.' Miss Holland rose now and after a reproving look in Alexandra's direction moved uncomfortably towards the door where Jason was standing. 'I expect we're all tired. I know I am.'

'I'm not,' declared Alexandra shortly, tipping her head on one side and daring Jason to argue with her, but he was already standing aside to allow her companion to leave the room.

'I suggest you rest for a while, Miss Holland,' he was saying with quiet assurance. 'Supper isn't served much before eight, and there's time for you to take a bath, if you'd like to.'

'Thank you. I may take you up on that,' she agreed, moving along the landing, and presently Alexandra heard the door of her room close behind her.

Only then did Jason step into her room, his face eloquent

with disapproval. 'Do you think you could refrain from embarrassing me in front of Miss Holland?' he demanded, in low angry tones, and her momentary joy that he had chosen to remain was quickly doused.

'Yes,' she declared now, holding up her chin, 'if you can guarantee that—that Estelita won't embarrass *me* in front of her!'

'Oh, God!' He raked back his hair with impatient fingers. 'Now what has she been saying?'

'Saying?' Alexandra's shrug was offhand. 'She hasn't exactly—said anything. It's just—her attitude,' she finished lamely.

'I see.' His lips thinned. 'Is that all?'

'No, it's not all.' Her chin jutted defensively. 'I like my room. It's very nice.' She paused. 'But I don't want to rest. I'm not tired. I want to see the ranch. I want to be with you!'

Jason's features took on the guarded expression she was coming to know so well. 'The *estancia*,' he said, stressing the Spanish derivative, 'comprises some twenty thousand acres. How much do you suppose you could see before it gets dark?' He gestured towards the open windows, where already shadows were falling. 'Tomorrow—or the next day —if you can sit a horse, I'll have Ricardo show you the home paddocks——'

'Ricardo!' Alexandra's chest heaved. 'I don't know Ricardo. I don't want Ricardo to show me the—the *estancia*. I want you——'

'*Alexandra!*' His use of her name cut her off in full spate. 'The sooner you realise your every wish is *not* my command, the better. All right, so I allowed you to come here as you wanted, but so long as you are living under my roof, there are certain things you will have to learn, and the first is that I cannot devote all my time to your entertainment!'

There was silence for a moment after that while they

viewed one another with wary speculation. Then Alexandra
spoke, but it was so quietly that he could barely hear the
words.

'You want me to hate it here, don't you?' she accused
him, in low choking tones. 'You want me to find it so awful
that I'll pack my bags and go away again, don't you? Then
you won't have to be bothered with me any longer!'

'Alexandra!' With a driven kind of anguish, he crossed
the room between them with long easy strides, and grasping her by the shoulders, he shook her until her head felt
too heavy for the slender column of her throat. 'Stop it!' he
ordered savagely. 'Stop feeling sorry for yourself. Of course
I want you here. If I hadn't, I wouldn't have allowed you
to come, whatever you said.'

'Is that true?' The long silky lashes swept upward, and
the smouldering torment of his gaze was achingly reassuring. 'Oh, Jason,' she whispered, lifting her hand to his face
and touching his cheek. 'Jason, you do care about me,
don't you?'

'I've said so, haven't I?' he muttered gruffly, but he held
himself away from her, and almost instinctively she moved
nearer to him.

Immediately she was aware of the tautness of his body,
of the moist male smell of him that no written word had
ever warned her about. She could feel the hard muscles of
his legs where hers were touching him, and longed, with an
incomprehensible yearning, for something she hardly understood; for some contact between them that was not compounded of sympathy and comfort.

'Jason . . .'

His name on her lips was a plea for understanding, but
when he turned his head and parted his lips against her
palm, she fairly snatched her hand away and pressed it
tightly to her. Her startled eyes were mesmerised by the
probing force of his, her whole body tingling with emotions
she was not equipped to handle. She felt her breasts taut
against the thinness of her vest, shameless in their eager-

ness, her head was swimming, and her legs, weak and trembling, scarcely had the strength to support her. Then she glimpsed the dawning cynicism in his gaze, the mocking curve of his mouth—and guessed his intention had been to achieve just this result. With a shudder of reaction, she pulled herself away from him, and his hands fell loosely to his sides.

'Yes,' he said, and his voice was low and angry, 'you are just a child, aren't you, Alexandra? So don't try to play the *femme fatale*. It doesn't satisfy.'

'I—I suppose you think I'm afraid of you!' she burst out jerkily, her arms folding about herself, as if for protection, and he nodded.

'Aren't you?' he demanded, and then, as if his patience had spent itself, he brushed past her and left the room.

CHAPTER THREE

THE mare was a solid little creature, with the gentlest eyes Alexandra had ever seen. Her colouring was not distinctive, a kind of rusty grey with spots of white splashed over her hindquarters, but compared to the horse they had had at the convent, she was a veritable thoroughbred. Alexandra was glad now she had spent so much time with the old shire horse at Sainte Sœur, grooming him and riding him, most times with only a blanket for a saddle.

Not that Ricardo had been convinced of her ability. He had had her ride the mare round and round the paddock until he assured himself that she was able to handle the animal, and her spine, still tender from the previous day's journey, ached from the unaccustomed exercise.

It was the morning after her arrival at San Gabriel, and Alexandra had awakened with a distinct feeling of discouragement. It was unusual for her, she was normally of an optimistic disposition, but she had lain for a few minutes recalling the events of the previous evening with depressing clarity.

After her confrontation with Jason she had felt little like eating supper, but a hasty bath, after Miss Holland had vacated the bathroom, and a change of clothes, had lightened her mood. It was too soon to jump to any conclusions, she had told herself firmly, flicking the skirt of an embroidered caftan down over her hips. Just because she and Jason had had their first row it did not mean that he was regretting bringing her here. They had had a difference of opinion, that was all—but deep inside her she had known it was more than that. At the first sign of his responding to the curious emotions he aroused inside her, she had bolted like a scared rabbit, and she was left with the disturbing evidence of her own immaturity.

Rummaging through her case—which had been brought by the same dark-skinned man who had provided Miss Holland's tray of tea—she had brought out the tattered copy of *Desert Rhapsody*, from which she had gleaned much of her knowledge of the man-woman relationship. It was most explicit in its descriptions of the torrid affair between a fragile English girl and a hawk-eyed Arab sheik, but although the girl shrank from the Arab's passions, the book never actually explained why. Indeed, the passions themselves were described in such a way that Alexandra scarcely understood what was going on. She only knew her imagination ran riot when Tarik 'tore the shimmering gauze from her slender body, and threw himself upon her', and there was an odd sensation in her lower limbs when she contemplated that intimate scene. It was strange, because the girl always gave in to the man, despite constant assertions that she hated him. Yet, as soon as he touched her, 'she was aflame'. Alexandra sighed and put the book away, and went down to supper with a rather thoughtful expression in her shadowed eyes.

They ate in what she assumed to be the dining room. It was a bare room, with a long low dresser set with plates, and an equally long table, covered by a linen cloth. Darkness had fallen, and the shutters had been drawn against the night insects, but their wings were still audible. They fought to reach the lamps that were standing at either end of the dresser, golden globes, that reminded Alexandra of the old oil lamps they used to use in the cellar at the convent. The lighting in the house was electric, however, and she had been surprised at this modern innovation in what was essentially a traditional dwelling.

As well as taking part in the serving of the meal, Estelita also ate with them, along with Ricardo Goya, and Pepe, the manservant who had brought their cases. Meeting Ricardo for the first time, Alexandra was rather intimidated by his enormous frame and grizzled dark hair, an extension of which grew down his cheeks and curled beneath his strong nose in exuberant *mostachos*. But his hearty laughter rang often in the high-ceilinged room, and his teasing baiting of Estelita made Alexandra his friend for life.

Pepe was a different proposition. A rather morose Jason had introduced the thin young man as Estelita's brother, and watching them together, Alexandra could see the resemblance. Both were very dark-skinned, although their features were predominantly Spanish, but Pepe's features were not quite so refined as his sister's. She was the older, too, possibly twenty-nine or thirty, Alexandra estimated, while Pepe was hardly more than her own age. He spoke little throughout the meal, and it was left to Estelita to question Jason about his journey, and Ricardo to make jokes at the housekeeper's expense.

All in all supper had not been a comfortable meal. Miss Holland had not joined them, after all, and Alexandra was very conscious of her own alienation among these people. She spent her time studying the relationships between them, avoiding the most obvious one between the man who persistently parried all questions, and the woman he called his housekeeper. Although from time to time, she sensed Pepe's eyes upon her, they dropped as soon as she lifted her head, and she came to the conclusion that he was intrigued by her pale skin. She had seen few pale-skinned people since coming to South America, but contrarily she admired the brown skins she had seen, envying them their immunity to the sun's rays.

Ricardo spoke to her once or twice, asking her about her father, and revealing that he, too, had known Charles Durham. It was reassuring to hear that her father was not forgotten by these men, but although she would have liked to have asked him questions, she was all too conscious of Estelita's cold dark eyes upon her.

The meal itself was rather too rich for her palate. A casserole of meat and vegetables, very highly spiced and hot with peppers, was an assault to a stomach still not attuned to the change of latitude, and Alexandra contented herself with crumbling the bread which accompanied it, and spreading it thinly with butter that tasted slightly rancid.

'You are not eating, *señorita*,' Estelita remarked once, her lips twisting contemptuously. 'She will never lose that boyish figure if she does not put some flesh on her bones, eh, Jason?'

Ricardo made a comment to this which seemed to amuse him greatly, and which caused the housekeeper's eyes to flash angrily. Her response was a vituperative tirade in their own language, which Jason silenced with a curt admonishment. But Ricardo was unrepentant, and turning to Alexandra, he explained:

'I tell Estelita she does not need any more flesh on her bones, no? I think perhaps she could afford to spare you some, hmm?'

'Ricardo!' Jason's impatient interjection gave Alexandra the chance to avoid an embarrassing answer, but Estelita was not appeased. She spent the remainder of the meal in sullen silence, only responding when Jason suggested she should serve the coffee.

Alexandra, apprehensive of Jason's censure, was glad when, after the meal was over, he disappeared, and making the excuse of seeing how Miss Holland was faring, she left the room. The hall was a silent cavern, and the lamp standing on the chest cast pools of darkness in shadowy corners. The remoteness of their situation was suddenly a tangible presence, and shivering slightly she crossed the tiled floor to the stairs. A shaft of light from an open doorway caught her gaze as she ascended the stairs and dipping slightly to peer into the room, she saw Jason standing behind a square desk. The desk was strewn with papers, and he was presently engrossed in the sheet he held in his hand, a brooding expression marring his lean features. His indifference to the isolation was reassuring somehow, but she went on her way, aware that for tonight at least, Jason's company was barred to her.

In her room, she turned out the light and stepped out on to the balcony. The scent from the passion-flower vine below her windows rose tantalisingly to her nostrils, and she tried to relax. But the starlit darkness was like a wall between her and the life she had known, and succumbing to a ridiculous sense of unease, she closed the shutters and went to find Miss Holland.

Morning had displaced the shadows of the night, and although it was early, even for her, Alexandra was up soon after six. Her system was still adjusting to the time change, and besides, she was eager to dispel her first impressions. She was sure her anxieties of the previous evening had been exaggerated, and the prospect of seeing more of the *estancia* lifted her spirits. She was even prepared to believe that that scene with Jason had never happened, that it had been some figment of her imagination, and she determined to show him that her feelings towards him had not changed. Exactly what those feelings were, she was not quite sure. She felt a sense of gratitude towards him, of course, but it was more than that that made her senses tingle when he was near her. He was much older than she was, even if he was much younger than her father had been, but not old enough to regard in that light. She only knew she liked being with him, better than with anyone she had ever known before, except perhaps her father, but even in her innocence she sensed that the relationship she wanted with Jason was much different from the relationship she had wanted with her father. It was all most disturbing. She had sent herself to sleep trying to imagine how she would feel if Jason treated her as the sheik had treated his fair prisoner, but her inexperienced imagination had been unable to provide any satisfactory answer.

After checking that Miss Holland was still sleeping, she went downstairs for breakfast. It was still barely seven, and she was glad of the warmth of cream cords and a matching

long-sleeved sweater. Her extreme fairness was accentuated
by the light-coloured clothes, and Pepe, encountering her
in the hall, stared with open eyes.

'Good morning,' she greeted him smilingly, but his
mumbled response was scarcely audible and she hurried
after him, saying: 'Where is everyone? Where's Jason? Is
he up?'

'*Por favor?*'

Pepe was obviously finding it difficult to follow her, and
Alexandra nodded her head, repeating slowly: 'Ja-son. Er—
donde es tá Jason?'

'Jason was up and out an hour ago,' remarked a supercilious voice behind her, and turning, Alexandra found
Estelita standing in the shadow of the stairs. 'You will need
to rise a little earlier to find him here, *señorita*.'

'I see.' Alexandra glanced back at Pepe and found him
shrugging as he went on his way.

'I did not know you spoke our language, *señorita*,' murmured the housekeeper mockingly. '*Deseaba usted algo?
Tiene usted hambre, acaso . . .*'

Alexandra controlled her temper with admirable restraint. 'You must know I do not speak Spanish, *señora*,'
she insisted quietly, but Estelita was not so willing to
abandon such a provocative subject.

'But you spoke in Spanish with my brother.'

'A word or two, only. I—well, I've heard Jason use those
words—when he asked about our luggage at the airport,
that's all.'

'Ah!' Estelita folded her arms across her ample bosom.
'You are very—what would you say?—sharp, no? I shall
have to be careful what I say when you are around,
señorita.'

Alexandra forced a smile, determining not to be pro-
voked, and as if her reaction was not what she had hoped,
Estelita's breath hissed a trifle impatiently as she swung
about and disappeared down a passage leading to the back
of the house. Giving herself a moment to school her

features, Alexandra followed her, and saw with interest that
the arched hallway overlooked the inner courtyard. A door
at the end of the passage was Estelita's destination, and
without giving herself time to have second thoughts, Alexandra went through the door after the housekeeper.

She found herself in a huge, old-fashioned kitchen that
was unpleasantly hot from the heat that emanated from an
enormous open grate. Despite an open door on to a yard
where chickens strutted, the temperature in the room was
suffocating, but Estelita seemed not to notice it. She
scarcely glanced at the girl who had followed her, before
going to the oven beside the fire and drawing out a tray of
loaves, golden brown and smelling deliciously. She set the
tray on the scrubbed pine table that occupied the centre of
the room, and then swung the oven door closed again with
her elbow.

Alexandra made another attempt to be civil. 'You make
all your own bread?' she asked, and the housekeeper bestowed on her a scornful stare.

'We have no shops here,' *señorita*. We cannot—how do
you say?—go to the supermarket, every time we want a
loaf, no?'

Alexandra pushed her hands into the hip pockets of her
cords. 'At the convent, we used to bake our own bread,
too,' she said. 'We couldn't afford the supermarket.'

'*Convento?*' Estelita echoed curiously. 'You were a
novicio?'

'Oh, no.' Alexandra's laugh was rueful. 'I just lived there.
I suppose it was a kind of boarding school. My father—my
father sent me there when I was very young.'

'Your father!' Estelita's moment of interest was gone.
'The man who made Jason responsible for his *son!*'

'No.' Alexandra shifted uncomfortably. 'No, actually,
that was me.'

'You?'

Estelita's lip curled, and Alexandra half wished she
hadn't been so honest. But it was too late now. 'Yes,' she

said. 'You see, my father always wanted a son, so he called me Alex. I—well, I naturally used that name ...'

'To trick Jason!' Estelita's eyes flashed. 'So you can come here, so you can make the nursemaid out of him!'

'No!' Alexandra was indignant. 'I'm not a child exactly.'

'No, you are not. So why are you not taking care of yourself?'

Alexandra heaved a sigh, looking about her helplessly, wishing Pepe would make a reappearance. 'Look,' she said, 'oughtn't you to take your complaints up with—with your employer?' She refused to say Jason to *her*! 'I—well, I'm hungry, as it happens. May I try some of your delicious-looking bread?'

Silently, Estelita supplied her with bread and butter, and a conserve made with peaches, which satisfactorily disguised the taste—which privately Alexandra thought had to be acquired—of the butter. There was coffee, too, strong and black, and highly aromatic, that completed a meal which, eaten in more congenial company, would have been very enjoyable.

Ricardo Goya appeared as she was finishing her second cup of coffee, and immediately Alexandra sensed the antagonism between these two. Ricardo greeted the housekeeper with a playful slap to her rump, as she bent over the basket of logs that fed the blaze, but her response was another of the vitriolic outbursts which had so marred supper the evening before.

Unrepentant, Ricardo turned to Alexandra, saying: 'So—and how is our visitor today? You did not sleep well, that you should be about so early?'

Alexandra rose to her feet. 'I expect it's because back in England the time would be ten or eleven o'clock,' she explained, rather awkwardly. 'I—er—I gather you've all been up for hours already.'

'Is that what *she* said?' Ricardo jerked his thumb in the housekeeper's direction, and then followed it with a dismissing motion. 'You do not think I would leave the comfort of my bed so early if I did not have to, do you?' He shook his head. 'No, but it is true. Jason and I were down at the stockyards by five-thirty. We are—how do you say? —putting the mark on the beef, no?'

'Branding?' asked Alexandra doubtfully, and Ricardo laughed and nodded.

'*Si*,' he said. 'Like this!' and he thrust a poker into the fire and brought it out smoking to lay across Estelita's back. The housekeeper jumped back angrily, and Alexandra's hand went to her lips in horror, but the foreman was only joking, and his amusement rang out once more.

'*Qué*, Estelita,' he exclaimed mockingly, 'you did not think I would brand *you, mi incendiaria?*'

Alexandra did not need a knowledge of the language to understand his meaning, and she was glad when he turned to her again and said:

'*Bueno*, if you are ready, *señorita*, my orders are to put myself at your disposal, *si?*'

'At *my* disposal?'

Alexandra, still scarcely recovered from his playful attack on Estelita, was taken aback, but Ricardo lounged against the table and said: '*Si*. You wish to see something of the *estancia*, do you not? Do you ride? If not, Jason says I must teach you.'

'You?'

Remembering what Jason had said, Alexandra ought not to have been surprised, but this man was so—overpowering. In leather leggings, and a sheepskin waistcoat over a brilliantly woven scarlet shirt, he was more like a gipsy than a rancher, and she wasn't at all sure she liked him any more than Estelita this morning.

'Come!' he said, and the housekeeper remarked: 'Yes, go, *señorita*. I do not like the smell of pigs in here.'

Ricardo's laughter had accompanied them outside, but once out of earshot of the house, he sobered and said apologetically: 'Do not take any notice of Estelita, *señorita*. She and I are old adversaries, *no?* Her husband was my best friend, but she never liked me. I think perhaps because I always could see the kind of woman she was.'

'Estelita is married?' exclaimed Alexandra, interested in her surroundings, but intrigued by his words.

'Not now, *señorita*,' he denied regretfully. 'Enrique is dead. *She* killed him. Oh, not actually . . .' This as Alexandra turned horrified eyes in his direction. 'But she is ambitious, *señorita*. She wanted money. And Enrique, poor fool, worked himself to death to keep her.'

Deciding this conversation had gone far enough, Alexandra pointed to the long wooden building ahead of them. 'I suppose that is where the men sleep, is it?'

Ricardo shrugged, and his good humour was restored. '*Si*,' he agreed. 'That is the bunkhouse, no? Come, I will introduce you to Chan.'

'Chan?'

'The cook. You did not think Estelita fed the men, too? No. They have their own cook, and a very fine one he is, too. My son lives with the men, and he vouches for his ability.'

He kissed the tips of his fingers as he spoke, and Alexandra felt herself relaxing. He could be so charming when he chose, and it was good to be out in the open air after the stifling heat of the kitchen.

They were crossing the yard that was bounded on two sides by outbuildings, but away to their left the pasture sloped towards the river. Stands of willow and poplar trees grew in clumps along the river bank, and Alexandra could see two riders on the far bank just sitting their horses, apparently lazing in the early morning sun. Beyond, the mist was slowly rising from the hills that circled the valley, and the sky was shading from apricot to palest yellow.

She was unaware of how expressive her features were until Ricardo bent his curly head to hers, and said, 'Is beautiful, *no*?' emotion for once overcoming his mastery of her language. But when Alexandra smiled, he realised his weakness and clapped a hand on her shoulder, almost

causing her to jump out of her skin. 'A hat,' he declared
gruffly, indicating her bare head. 'With such pale skin, you
must always wear a hat. I will get you one.'

Adjoining the long bunkhouse, which lay beyond the
storehouses, was the cookhouse. It was a squarer building,
built of logs, notched at the corners and painted with
creosote for waterproofing; it provided cooking and eating
facilities for the men who worked on the *estancia*, with
plenty of room for casual workers when they were hired.
Most of the cooking was done on a huge, log-fired range,
but there was a gas cooker for emergency use. Long wooden
tables were lined with benches, and empty now, it smelled
of the burnt steaks the men had had for breakfast. It was
not an unpleasant smell, mingling as it did with coffee and
tobacco smoke, and Alexandra really felt as if she was learning something about her new surroundings.

Chan, as she had expected, was Chinese, but she guessed
his parentage had been mixed. He was taller than the
average Chinese, and his eyes were not as narrow. Like
Ricardo, he had an ample girth, which said much for his
own food, and his smile was seldom long absent from his
olive-skinned features.

'Miss Tarrant,' he said politely, when she was introduced
to him, which evoked another of Ricardo's hearty laughs.

'She is not Jason's daughter, Chan!' he exclaimed with
humour. 'Does she look like him, I ask you? No, her father
was the good friend to the *patrón*, *si*?'

'Ah!' Chan nodded. 'Well, I am happy to meet you,
señorita,' he added, with a distinctly American intonation.
'You think you will like it here?'

'I hope so,' Alexandra smiled. 'I like what I've seen so
far.'

'That includes you, Chan,' jeered Ricardo, with his usual
humour, but the Chinese cook took it in good part.

'You'd like to stay for coffee?' he suggested, indicating
the pot on the polished range, but Ricardo shook his head
now.

'The *señorita* is going to show me if she can ride,' he
declared, and Alexandra wasn't sure whether he was mocking her or not. 'You can come and watch, Chan. You know
a good *gaucho* when you see one.'

'Oh, but . . .' Alexandra licked her lips doubtfully, sure
she would make a fool of herself on any horse Ricardo chose
to produce, and Chan shook his head.

'Some other time, Rico,' he promised, and with a chuckle,
the foreman followed her outside again.

The stables were nearby, and here Alexandra was introduced to the elderly Indian whose job it was to keep the
stalls clean and the brasses polished. There were saddles
hanging on the walls, big, cumbersome saddles, which she
hadn't the first idea how to fasten, but Ricardo ignored
them.

The little mare he produced for her was a docile creature,
much different from the stallion in the adjoining stall, who
whinnied protestingly when they ignored him. The mare's
name was Placida, and Alexandra could see why, although
she felt her first misgivings when Ricardo threw only a
sheepskin fleece across the mare's back before leading her
outside. Hanging by the door were several of the broad-
brimmed sombreros she had seen men wearing in Valvedra,
and Ricardo planted one of these on her head before she
emerged into the sunlight.

'I—er—don't we need a saddle?' she asked, as her companion adjusted the bridle over the mare's ears, and he
grinned.

'First I see how you sit the horse,' he said. She had told
him about the horse at the convent on their way to the
stables. 'Then we will see about a saddle, *no?*'

Adjusting the hat on her head, Alexandra accepted his
hand to mount the animal, the sheepskin a comforting
barrier between her spine and the mare's back. She took
the reins he handed to her, dug in her heels, and Placida
walked obediently forward. Immediately, her sombrero
went flying back off her head, and as she twisted in an

attempt to retrieve it, the sheepskin beneath her slid sideways, and she would have fallen to the ground if Ricardo's
strong arms had not caught her.

He set her on her feet, rescued the hat, and then directed
her to tie the cords beneath her chin. 'Right,' he said, when
this was done to his satisfaction, offering his linked fingers
for her foot. 'Shall we begin again?'

An hour later he had satisfied himself that she would
not fall off again, but Alexandra's legs felt like jellies as she
clambered down.

'Qué?' Ricardo regarded her with humour. 'Do you not
wish to go riding after all?'

Her spine smarting from the hardness of the mare's,
Alexandra regarded him with ill-concealed resentment.
'You know I'm aching all over!' she accused, half tearfully.
'Why couldn't I have used a saddle like anyone else?'

Ricardo's features softened. 'Don't you know that in
country like this, it is always best to learn the hard way?
To ride without a saddle is an achievement. It means you
are controlling the horse from here ...' He indicated his
knees. 'Bodily contact, no? Now, you will never forget what
you have learned. You know the feel of the animal. The
touch, no?'

Touching! Again that word, thought Alexandra ruefully.
She thought if anyone touched her spine ever again, she
would scream in agony.

'So?' Ricardo smiled encouragingly. 'You will forgive the
lesson, hmm?'

'Oh, yes. Yes.' Alexandra sniffed, half regretting her
anger with him. 'I—I suppose I should—thank you.'

'Thank me?' Ricardo laughed. 'Why? For hurting you?
No, no.' He shook his head. 'But look, is not this the elderly
lady you brought with you?'

'Miss Holland?'

Alexandra swung round, a finger raised to her lips in
dismay, as she realised she had forgotten all about her

companion. Miss Holland, ridiculously out of place in country tweeds and stout brogues, was marching across the paddock towards them, and Ricardo bent his head to whisper outrageously: 'Shall we teach the lady how to ride, too? I could lend her some pants, and a shirt, *no?*'

Ignoring him, although her lips twitched irresistibly, Alexandra walked painfully to meet the other woman. Her somewhat mincing steps did not go unobserved, and Miss Holland looked first at her, and then past her to the grinning black-haired giant behind her.

'Alexandra!' she exclaimed in alarm, and almost at the same moment Alexandra realised she probably looked as rough as she felt. The sombrero had slipped to the back of her neck, and her hair was a tumbled mass about her shoulders, her cream cords stained from the sweat of the mare's sides.

'Hello, Miss Holland,' she said. 'I'm sorry if you've been concerned about me. But as you can see——'

'What have you been doing with yourself?' Miss Holland spoke to her, but she was looking at Ricardo, and with his usual showmanship, he swept her a deep bow, stepping forward and saying:

'I have been giving your young friend a riding lesson, *señora*. Regrettably, she has—how do you say?—overdone it, *no?*'

'Overdone it? Overdone what?' Miss Holland was not in a mood to be placated so easily, and Alexandra sighed before explaining that her back was aching from the exercise.

'And in this heat!' exclaimed Miss Holland when she had finished. 'Do you want to be taken ill as soon as you arrive?'

It was only as she said this that Alexandra began to realise how warm it had become, and feeling her damp forehead, she guessed her face was streaked with sweat, too.

'Don't you realise how susceptible you are in a strange climate?' Miss Holland persisted, but Alexandra waved her protests aside.

'Have you met Ricardo?' she asked, knowing full well she hadn't, and their introduction successfully halted any further objections on Miss Holland's part. Instead, Ricardo took his cue and insisted on introducing the lady to the mare, and because she was such a gentle animal, Miss Holland was diverted.

But later, when she and Alexandra walked back to the house together, she returned to the attack. 'I must say, I was surprised to hear that Mr Tarrant had suggested Señor Goya as your instructor. The man looks scarcely civilised. Is he an Indian, do you think? He has a very large nose.'

'Indians don't usually wear hair on their faces,' said Alexandra thoughtfully, remembering something she had read years ago. Certainly, the Indian in the painting at the convent had not had any hair on his face, and thinking of the Indian brought irresistible thoughts of Jason.

Shading her eyes, she looked across the valley, but it was too long and too wide to allow her to see anything more than the sweeping stretch of grassland, and the blue-grey curve of the river where it reflected the arc of the sky. She could see a pall of dust in the distance, which could mean anything, but all she could hear were the domestic sounds of the beasts in the pasture near the *hacienda* and the continual clucking of the hens.

From this side, the house looked different, set about with its pens and outbuildings. The store-sheds, Ricardo had told her, contained everything necessary to a community of this size, including animal feedstuffs, and farm machinery, crockery and leather goods, and dried food and meat enough for a siege. There was a smithy, he had told her, at the stockyards, and sheds for shearing the sheep that ran the high ranges, but the *hacienda* itself was the kingpin by which the *estancia* was controlled, the axle on which the various spokes of life at San Gabriel turned.

She wondered if Jason would return for the midday meal, but in this she was disappointed. The meal which was served, much to Miss Holland's distaste, at the kitchen table, was attended by Estelita, Pepe and themselves, Ricardo having disappeared about his own business. Alexandra guessed her companion found life at the *hacienda* much different to what she was used to, and she spared a moment to wonder what Jason would do should Miss Holland choose to pack her bags and return to England. It was always possible that she might find the heat, or the isolation, or even Estelita's familiarity more than she could take, and decide that however difficult her circumstances, life in England was preferable to this remote valley. Whatever else she was, Miss Holland was first and foremost a gentlewoman, and the crude humour of men like Ricardo Goya could only accentuate the distinctions.

Sighing, Alexandra tried to concentrate on the meat-filled pancake in front of her. She must not think so pessimistically. After all, Miss Holland had been told the circumstances of life out here before she left England. The fact that it was different from what either of them had imagined did not mean it was going to prove unacceptable to them.

CHAPTER FOUR

IT was the next morning before Alexandra encountered Jason again.

Following her riding lesson, she found she was very tired, and although she forced herself to go down for supper, the fact that only herself and Estelita were present might have saved her the trouble. The housekeeper took great pleasure in informing her that Jason had sent a message to the effect that it would be late before he got back, and even Pepe had deserted the supper table to join the men in the bunkhouse. Alexandra had seen the men returning earlier in the evening, the thunder of their horses' hooves bringing her to the balcony doors. But straight from the bath, and only thinly clad in a silk wrapper, she had quickly disguised herself behind the curtains, just in case anyone should come her way. She had expected Jason to be with them, and it was with an acute feeling of disappointment that she listened to Estelita's mocking explanation.

Miss Holland had done as she had the night before, and been served her meal in her room. She was feeling the heat and the change of latitude, too, and Alexandra herself had approved her choice. However, when she found she had only Estelita for company, she dearly wished the older woman had joined them, after all.

They ate a concoction of beef, black beans and rice, and Alexandra couldn't decide whether she found its spicy mixture more acceptable because her stomach had adjusted to the flavour, or simply because she was anxious and she was eating to compensate. Whatever, she parried Estelita's more pointed questions, and succeeded in getting the woman to talk about herself. Estelita, it turned out, was of Portuguese extraction and had been born in Sao Paulo. Although she and Pepe were brother and sister, they had had different fathers, Pepe's father having lived in Valvedra all his life. It was there that Estelita's mother had met him when her first husband had deserted her, she said. She didn't say a lot about her father. Apparently, she hardly remembered him; and also, she didn't explain what her mother was doing in Valvedra while her father was reputedly looking for work elsewhere. However, it seemed that Pepe's father's advent had been the turning point in all their lives, and she and Pepe were very close. She did not mention her own husband, or the fact that he was dead.

It was only towards the end of the meal that she seemed to realise she had done all the talking, but by then Alexandra was too tired to respond to her deliberate baiting.

Her offer of help with the washing up being rejected, Alexandra left the room after the meal and sought the sanctuary of her bedroom. During the afternoon, she had explored a little more of the house, and knew that there was a comfortable *salón* adjoining the room she thought of as Jason's study, but this evening it had no appeal. She knew if she sat there in solitary state she would fall asleep, and she didn't want Jason to come upon her snoring or, horror of horrors, with her mouth open. Besides, he would not expect her to wait up, he might not even want her to wait up, and Estelita was waiting in the kitchen, like some jealous spider, in her web.

As if to compensate for her tiredness the night before, the next morning, Alexandra was awake as soon as it was light. Expecting some hangover from the previous day's riding lesson, she was pleasantly surprised to find that apart from a little stiffness, she felt fine, and even eager to get into the saddle again . . . or its equivalent.

Collecting her spongebag, she went along to the bathroom, expecting it to be empty at this hour of the morning, and walked straight in on Jason, sluicing his neck at the basin.

'Oh, I—I'm sorry,' she began, awkward at this unexpected encounter. 'I mean—Estelita said you usually—showered . . .'

Jason had grabbed a towel and draped it round his neck as she spoke. He was bare to his waist, the denim pants he wore hanging low on his hips. But it was the jagged scratch that ran the length of his arm from elbow to wrist that caught her attention as he turned, and her lips parted in anxious question. Seeing her immediate reaction, he pulled a wry face, saying dryly:

'That's why I didn't take a shower this morning. I decided I'd better wash in filtered water until it heals over.'

'But it should be stitched!' she protested, forgetting for the moment that she was wearing only the cotton nightshirt she had worn to sleep in, and going towards him. Her tentative fingers reached out to touch the bruised area around the gash, trembling against his warm flesh. 'How did you do it? It's so deep!'

Jason removed her fingers firmly and finished drying his neck. 'It will heal,' he asserted flatly. 'A rogue steer decided he'd put his own brand on me, that's all. I'll live, I can assure you.'

'Oh, but Jason, it should have proper treatment,' she exclaimed, not responding to the warning light in his eyes. 'Don't you have any medication—bandages?'

Jason reached for his shirt, which was lying on the chair beside the bath. 'Are you a nurse, too?' he enquired derisively, his mouth pulling down at the corners, but she paid no attention to his sarcasm.

'I've treated cuts,' she defended, her lips pursed. 'Do you want to get septicaemia? Would you like to lose an arm?'

'My God, you're a little pessimist, aren't you?' he exclaimed, but he hesitated before pulling on his shirt. It was then she saw the shirt he had discarded, dropped in the bath, caked with dried blood.

'Jason, please,' she pleaded. 'Let me put some ointment on it for you. Surely a bandage won't—cramp your style.'

'I'll get Estelita to do it,' he said, bending to pick up the soiled shirt, and she could have stamped her foot in frustration.

'Why can't I?'

Jason straightened, and his features had taken on a resigned expression. 'I thought we went into all that,' he observed quietly, but she didn't respond. 'All right,' he said, after another moment's silence, 'I'll put some ointment on it myself. I have a case of liniment in my room, and I believe there's some Savlon there, too.'

Alexandra said nothing. She just stood aside when he went past her, and then, putting down her sponge bag, she followed him.

Jason's room was several doors along the landing from her own, above the curve of the staircase. She guessed it was the master bedroom, judging by the size of the bed that occupied the centre of the room. Unlike her bed, it had hanging drapes, and the curtains and coverings were predominantly brown. But it was just as starkly furnished, except for the pictures on the walls.

She was hovering at the doorway when he saw her. He had pulled a drawer open in the chest beside the long windows, and was attempting to wind a length of bandage about his wrist. It was an impossible task, and the words he was muttering to himself were not words the nuns would have approved of.

'What do you want?' he demanded, as she stood there, and she stepped into the room, gesturing that she could apply the dressing.

'And what do you suppose Miss Holland would say if she came by and saw you in my bedroom dressed like that?' Jason asked irritably, making her aware for the first time that she was still in her nightshirt.

Then, determined not to appear naïve, she said: 'I'm adequately covered, aren't I? If I were wearing a bikini——'

'But you're not, are you?' Jason retorted. 'And this is

not the beach. Oh—what the hell, all right. Help me. But be quick about it.'

Alexandra approached him cautiously, but with the roll of bandage in her hand, she felt more confident. However, winding it about his arm brought her close to his lean, muscled body, and every now and then her fingers brushed the skin of his midriff. Although he had smeared some ointment over the cut which had successfully stopped the bleeding, it was still an ugly sight, and she knew the most ridiculous impulse to comfort him. But he didn't want her sympathy, and she had to content herself with making the best job of it that she could.

'You're very efficient,' he murmured, as she reached his elbow and tore the bandage down the middle for a few inches to bind it with a knot. Then, his breath whistling unevenly in his throat, he added: 'I haven't seen you since the night you arrived. Are you settling down?'

Alexandra finished the job, but she didn't immediately move away from him. 'I expect so,' she answered quietly, running her fingers down the ridges of the bandage. 'Does that feel too tight?'

'It feels just fine,' he assured her, and she nodded her head with satisfaction. 'I hear Ricardo gave you quite a riding lesson yesterday.'

She half smiled at that. 'Did he tell you? I fell off once.'

'You did?' Jason's brows descended. 'Were you hurt?' His mouth tightened. 'He didn't tell me that.'

'Oh, it was nothing,' she exclaimed, shaking her head. 'It was my own fault. And he caught me.'

'Did he?' Jason's voice was rough. 'Well, take more care in future.'

'I will.' She dimpled. 'It's nice to know you care.'

'I care,' he agreed curtly. Then: 'I have to go. Estelita will be waiting with my breakfast.'

'Oh!' Alexandra's parted lips revealed her disappointment. 'You're not going down to the stockyards again!'

'Not this morning, no. I want to drive over to Puerto

Novo to collect some stores for Chan.' He paused. 'Why? Do you want to come?'

'Could I?'

Alexandra gazed up at him in delight, and as if regretting his impulsive invitation, Jason grimaced. 'I guess so,' he conceded, reaching for his shirt, but she forestalled him, wrapping her arms around his waist and hugging him.

'Thank you,' she breathed, pressing her lips to the hair-roughened skin of his chest, and then putting out her tongue as the fine filaments tickled her nose.

'Alexandra . . .' His impatient protest accompanied his hands gripping her upper arms, pushing her back from him. But the thoughtless action sent a shaft of pain ripping up his arm to his shoulder, and he uttered an involuntary groan, releasing her abruptly.

'Oh, your arm!' she gasped in dismay. 'Jason—I'm sorry . . .'

'Forget it,' he gritted, between his teeth, but his face was pale under his tan.

'I can't forget it,' she persisted. 'It—it was my fault. If I hadn't been so careless . . .'

'I said it's all right,' he muttered, but there were beads of sweat standing out on his forehead, and she saw the tell-tale stains seeping through the white bandage.

'It's not all right,' she argued. 'It's started bleeding again.'

'*God!*' His frustration caused a pulse to throb revealingly near his jawline, and Alexandra, thinking his anger was caused by the re-opening of the injury, started to unwind the bandage. He stopped her with his uninjured arm, grasping both her hands in one of his, and saying tautly: 'What the hell do you think you're doing now?'

'I—I was going to dress the wound again,' she stammered, but the ugly oath he uttered silenced her.

'And what then?' he demanded. 'After the wound is dressed to your satisfaction, what then? Will you kiss it better?'

Alexandra caught her breath at the glittering fire of his eyes. 'If—if you want me to,' she ventured chokingly, but he flung her hands from him with such force that she almost fell.

'You—are—a—menace!' he grated, enunciating each word with heavy significance. 'Do you know that? Oh, go on—get out of here. I'll do it myself.'

'But, Jason——'

'I said go!'

She caught her lower lip between her teeth. 'Will you—will you still take me to Puerta Nova?' she ventured, as he regarded her without liking.

'Puerto Novo,' he corrected irritably. Then, with a harsh exclamation he nodded. 'Yes. Yes, I'll take you. And Miss Holland, too, if she'd like to come.'

'Miss Holland?'

Alexandra couldn't hide her dismay, but Jason's hand in the small of her back propelled her purposefully towards the door. 'Yes, Miss Holland,' he agreed. 'Ask her!' And she had no alternative but to obey.

In the doorway, however, his voice stopped her, and she turned eagerly, her spirits lifting, sure he had changed his mind.

But his expression was not encouraging, and his: 'Put some clothes on before you ask her, won't you?' was not what she wanted to hear. Cheeks burning, she walked quickly back to her room.

Puerto Novo was a small town, situated in the mountains, midway between Valvedra and Montesanto, the western state capital. It was accessible from the coast by the railway that had been built many years before, and Jason explained that it was from here that his beef cattle began their journey east. It was half a day's journey from San Gabriel, through some of the most rugged scenery Alexandra had ever seen, but again she was in the back of the Range-Rover and at the mercy of every pothole in the road.

Miss Holland had chosen to join them after all. Privately, Alexandra didn't blame her not wanting to spend the day in Estelita's company, particularly as the housekeeper had made no secret of her dislike of the arrangement. Not that she had actually said anything in Alexandra's presence, but the malevolent looks she cast in Jason's direction were enough, signifying as they did the words that had passed between them.

Apart from holding his arm a little stiffly, Jason showed no sign of his injury, but Alexandra couldn't help but notice how the muscles in his face tautened when they bumped over a particularly rough patch of ground. She was concerned about the dangers of infection in an area like this, but she refrained from voicing her opinion in Miss Holland's company.

For the most part, Jason spoke to Miss Holland during the journey, inviting her opinion of the *estancia*, encouraging her to air any grievances she might be feeling. Was her room comfortable? Was the food to her liking? Did she think she would get used to the remoteness and the isolation?

Miss Holland was reticent. Her room was very pleasant, she said, and the bed was extremely comfortable. But the food was obviously very different from what she was used to, and so far as the remoteness and isolation were concerned, she hadn't yet had the time to come to any decision.

'I'm hoping Alexandra and I will get about a little more freely when she has mastered the art of riding,' she said, causing the girl's lips to part in astonishment, and even Jason glanced at her a trifle disbelievingly.

'You—ride, Miss Holland?' he asked politely, and she nodded.

'Reasonably well,' she agreed. 'When I was tutoring Lord Carleon's children, we spent a considerable amount of time at his estate in Ireland. Naturally, the children learned to ride, it was expected of them, and I accompanied them.'

Jason uttered an amused chuckle. 'Well, well! Hidden talents. My apologies, Miss Holland. I should have known a little thing like sitting a horse wouldn't be beyond your capabilities.' He glanced round at his ward, sitting in glum incredulity in the back. 'Do you hear that, Alexandra? You and Ricardo will have companionship on your outings. I shan't need to feel that I'm neglecting you, if Miss Holland is along.'

Alexandra said nothing, but the challenge in her gold-fringed violet eyes did not go unobserved. However, Jason seemed more interested in finding out more about his un-usual middle-aged companion, and for the rest of the journey Alexandra viewed the scenery with a slightly jaundiced eye. She had expected she and Jason would take rides together. She had looked forward to him showing her over the *estancia*. But now, it seemed, they would have Miss Holland's company, too, and like today, Alexandra would be pushed into the background. The fact that this wasn't strictly true, that Alexandra herself had suggested Miss Holland should sit in front, was forgotten. Instead, she stared gloomily out on to rolling plateaux and mountain peaks which had somehow lost their appeal.

Puerto Novo was quite a busy metropolis. As they neared the town, they passed more houses and homesteads, and there was a little traffic on the road, including some of the ox-drawn carts that Alexandra had found so picturesque in the outlying villages surrounding Valvedra. The carts were piled high with fruit and vegetables, no doubt bound for the market, and her mouth watered at the sight of huge peaches, downy-soft and juicy, bouncing along beside oranges and melons, and luscious bunches of grapes.

The town itself was situated round a square where the parish church of St Cecilia faced the municipal buildings. The church itself dated from the eighteenth century, Jason told them after he had parked the Range-Rover in a street close by, and he recommended a visit if they had the time. But it was almost lunchtime, and he suggested they have a meal in the hotel before going about their separate pursuits. Alexandra, who had expected to stay with him, suppressed the protest that rose to her lips at this information, and was unusually silent over the meal of *asado criollo*, barbecued meat, which was served with a delicious side salad. She refused anything but fruit to finish, and watched without amusement as Miss Holland ploughed her way through a particularly sticky pastry, coated with raisins and sugar. They drank *mate*, the local tea, and Jason smoked one of his long cigars, and then he suggested the 'ladies' might like to go shopping while he completed his business.

'Does that appeal to you, Alexandra?' asked Miss Holland, turning to her charge, but Alexandra only shrugged. The question was largely academic anyway, as her opinion was not consulted with any real purpose, and she refused to respond to the warning impatience in Jason's expression.

'Is that what you want to do, Alexandra?' he asked, virtually repeating Miss Holland's words, and she raised her shoulders in a gesture of indifference.

'Whatever you arrange,' she said, with pointed candour, and he thrust his hands into the pockets of his pants, as if not trusting himself not to shake her.

'I want to go to the bank, and there are various men I have to see,' he said, speaking through his teeth, for her benefit alone. 'Now if you think standing around listening to me arguing about my overdraft, or discussing the trade in hides, is more interesting than spending a couple of hours looking round the shops——'

'I do!' she declared, overriding him. 'I'm not an inveterate window-shopper. I only go shopping if there's something I want to buy.'

Jason's frustration was evident. 'Well, you can't come with me,' he averred harshly. 'At the risk of sounding pompous, my business affairs are private. I don't want you butting in.'

'You do sound pompous!' retorted Alexandra, hiding the hurt in her voice. 'Pompous and—and dull! I don't want to listen to your stupid old private affairs. I wouldn't know what you were talking about anyway, would I?'

'Then you'll go with Miss Holland, and accompany her on her shopping trip,' commanded Jason coldly, his patience shredding. 'I'll see you both back here at four o'clock!' And he strode away before she could make any further objections.

After he had gone there was an unpleasant silence for a few moments, then Miss Holland said: 'That was rather childish, wasn't it, Alexandra? What on earth possessed you to speak to Mr Tarrant like that?'

Realising Miss Holland was unaware of the development of their relationship, Alexandra sighed. After all, it was hardly the woman's fault if Jason chose to behave as if she was some annoying child throwing a temper tantrum. And it had been childish to behave as she had, she knew that. But—dear God! he made her act that way, behaving as if she was incapable of looking after herself.

It seemed that every time she and Jason came to words, she lost the battle. She didn't have his experience, of course, and he could always patronise her. But there were times when she sensed he enjoyed her company—and resented it. It was as if he had constantly to remind himself that she was only seventeen—well, nearly eighteen, she amended, remembering it was only four months to her birthday. Or maybe she was completely wrong. Maybe he only acted that way sometimes. Was he acting on the occasions when he was nice to her, and not on the occasions when he was brutal? One thing was certain, he had the almost exclusive ability to hurt her, and used it, indiscriminately.

Miss Holland was still waiting for a reply, and pulling herself together with an effort, Alexandra made a moue with her lips. 'He—annoys me,' she said lamely. 'I didn't realise he was bringing us here to abandon us.'

Miss Holland clicked her tongue. 'My dear child, a man with Mr Tarrant's responsibilities can't be expected to take time off to entertain us. You have to remember that we're the outsiders here, that without your father's intervention, you wouldn't even be in Mr Tarrant's care. I think his taking it upon himself to place you in his personal care until your eighteenth birthday is commendable, but you mustn't expect too much of him. He has his own life to lead, and we must just—fit ourselves to his plans.'

The words Alexandra would have liked to have offered in response to that little speech trembled on her tongue, but she was learning caution. Behaving like a shrew was not going to achieve anything. And yet submitting to his admonitions as if they were unworthy of contradiction was totally alien to her beliefs. At the convent, she had been taught that the truth was all, that telling lies or dissembling was wrong. Yet already she had learned that being honest earned one a reputation for childishness, and showing her feelings had aroused anger and impatience.

In the event, the afternoon passed quite pleasantly. Miss Holland was soon bored with the limitations of shopping on the Avenida Central, and instead, they explored the gardens of the memorial erected to a famous freedom fighter, and visited the church. The screens that flanked the altar were exquisitely painted, and there were real gems in the robes of the Virgin, whose statue dominated the Lady Chapel. Saint Cecilia herself was depicted in the panes of the stained-glass windows that distributed the sun's rays in multi-faceted colours across polished wooden pews.

Jason was already waiting for them when they arrived back at the hotel. He had ordered tea, and listened with interest while Miss Holland described their afternoon. Alexandra said little, but she did observe that he was holding his arm more stiffly, and unable to prevent the words, asked how it was.

Miss Holland looked surprised at the question, unaware as she was of the injury, and Jason's mouth turned down at the corners as he admitted that he had seen a doctor and had a couple of shots. Alexandra, feeling justifiably relieved, couldn't prevent a smug smile from appearing on her lips as he explained to Miss Holland what had happened.

'My goodness!' she exclaimed, pressing her lace handkerchief to her lips. 'You could have been killed!'

'Hardly,' remarked Jason dryly. 'Alexandra exaggerates its importance. It's only a scratch. I stood more danger from the infection than from the wound itself.'

'Even so . . .' Miss Holland shook her head, and Alexandra faced him with defiant eyes. After all, he had seen a doctor, as she had suggested, and that proved something, didn't it?

The journey back to San Gabriel was more hairy than the outward journey had been. For one thing, shadows were lengthening, casting veils of shade across the road, and the winking sensation of the sun darting at them between the leaves of the trees had a stroboscope effect. For another, Jason drove more swiftly, not taking his time as he had on the way to Puerto Novo, so that they could enjoy the scenery. It was growing late, and he wanted to get back before total darkness engulfed them. Alexandra could understand that. She had already experienced how total that darkness could be. Nevertheless, she wished she could forget the fact that in places the road skirted stark ravines and precipices, a narrow track winding its precarious way through the mountains.

Both she and Miss Holland breathed a sigh of relief when the lights of the *hacienda* became visible ahead of them, and Alexandra leant forward in her seat for the last few minutes, surprised at the sense of homecoming she felt. Her arm rested companionably on Jason's shoulder and this time he didn't draw away, a fact which made her wish they had more than just a few hundred yards to go.

CHAPTER FIVE

Miss Holland wore jodhpurs for riding, uncomfortably heavy breeches, that looked totally out of place in such surroundings. She also insisted on wearing a riding hat, instead of the sombrero Ricardo offered, and her appearance was not unreminiscent of the final days of the Indian Raj. Nevertheless, her ability could not be faulted, and the protection afforded by the helmet was undeniable. She became quite a well-known figure about the *estancia*, and the men called her *La Mula*, because she was so stubborn. Not that she seemed to object. She had their reluctant respect, too, and the men had names for all of them. Alexandra was always referred to as *La Niña*, and while she didn't care for the childish overtones, she knew it was a form of endearment.

Ricardo mounted Miss Holland on a grey gelding, and Alexandra graduated to a chestnut mare, several hands taller than Placida. She found the more she rode, the more confidence she gained, and during the week that followed the three of them ventured further and further afield. Surprisingly, after their initial antagonism was spent, Miss Holland and Ricardo became quite good friends, his derision giving way to admiration as she proved the horsewoman she was.

During these days Alexandra saw next to nothing of Jason. He spent most of the day out of the house, and after supper in the evening, he retired to his study to continue working. He worked hard, she acknowledged that, as hard as any of the men he employed, and involved himself in every aspect of the running of the *estancia*. Because he was an engineer, he had been able to put his technical skills to good use, and Ricardo had told them how he had installed the plumbing system at the house himself. He had also dug new wells to replace the dried-up waterholes used by the cattle, and consequently a long dry spell no longer meant animals dying of thirst, and enabled them to increase their numbers.

The *estancia* itself was huge. Alexandra believed Ricardo when he said it took several days to ride around the outer boundaries of the property, and how, at the yearly round-up, the men were forced to sleep rough during the long trail. She thought she would like to sleep rough, under the stars, making supper over the campfire. It was a romantic notion, and she paid little heed to Ricardo's jeers about snakes and lizards and poisonous spiders.

It was during one of their morning rides that she saw the black stallion again. They had taken the trail into the mountains, and came upon a herd of horses grazing together in one of the grassy gorges that fed the river. Their advent caused some nervousness among the animals, and Alexandra was so entranced by the sight of so many horses together that she didn't at first see the glossy black ears flattened in warning of their approach. By the time she did see him, the herd was already moving, the thunder of their hooves vibrating within the walls of the canyon.

'Qué diablo!' grunted Ricardo impatiently, as they disappeared from view. 'He is an arrogant devil, that one! He has the pride of Lucifer himself.'

'Are they wild?' asked Alexandra, still bemused by what she had seen, but Ricardo shook his head.

'There are no wild horses in Santa Vittoria,' he said. 'They are all descendants from a shipment of horses from Paraguay, left to run free on the *pampas*. The herd you have just seen belongs to the *patrón*, and like the cattle, they are rounded up every year and the surplus sold.'

'And—and the stallion?'

Ricardo laughed. 'That black bastard? He is a selfish beast, that one. He keeps all the mares for himself.'

'Jason said the Indians regard him as—sacred.'

'Some do. Some don't. The truth is, they are a—how do you say?—superstitious people. Because no one has been able to stay on his back long enough to break him to the saddle, he has become a *legendario, no*?'

'A legend?' Alexandra translated, smiling. 'But a nice legend, isn't it?'

'Except when we have to round up the mares,' amended Ricardo dryly. 'He knows every ravine and gully in these mountains, every pass, every canyon. It is the work of the devil to find them.'

Alexandra nodded, pushing back the brim of her hat, the sun warm on her thinly-clad shoulders. Already its rays had added a creamier texture to her skin, and this morning, to her horror, she had found freckles on her nose. As if remembering this, she pulled the brim forward again to shadow her face, and followed Miss Holland's broad back as they turned for home.

That evening over supper Alexandra spoke again of the black stallion, and was surprised when Jason raised dark eyebrows at Ricardo and said sharply: 'I thought you promised me you wouldn't ride into the mountains.'

There was anger as well as curtness in his tones, and Alexandra was surprised when Ricardo made a kind of half hearted apology. 'We did not go far, *patrón*,' he protested. 'We were never in any danger.'

'Danger?' Miss Holland, who invariably joined them for the evening meal now, looked astonished. 'We—that is, Alexandra and I—are both competent riders, Mr Tarrant. I don't think you need to worry about us.'

'Ricardo knows my orders, ma'am,' retorted Jason politely. 'For the present, I would prefer you to stay nearer the homestead.'

Miss Holland sniffed her disapproval, and attacked the beef and vegetables on her plate with more aggression than enthusiasm. Alexandra was puzzled too, half wishing she hadn't brought up their sighting of the black horse, but unlike her companion she said nothing, aware of Estelita's mocking amusement at the little affray. However, when Jason left the table some minutes later, she made a hasty excuse and followed him, surprised to find him on the point of going out the main door. She had thought he was on his way to his study, and she hesitated a moment before speaking his name. He turned abruptly, his expression thoughtful, and her mouth went dry as the words she had meant to use deserted her.

'Yes?' he said, and she thought she detected a certain wariness about his response.

'I—where are you going?' she asked, although she had not meant to ask that at all, and his mouth twisted.

'Would you believe—for a walk?' he enquired sardonically, and she took an involuntary step forward.

'May I come with you?'

Jason sighed. 'Don't you usually play chess with Miss Holland in the evenings?'

Alexandra didn't realise he had noticed. 'I do—sometimes,' she conceded, 'but Ricardo plays, too, and he gives her a much better game than I do.'

Jason looked down at his booted feet for a moment, and then lifted his eyes to her face again. 'All right,' he said, although his voice was clipped. 'But don't you need a coat?'

Alexandra was wearing an ankle-length gown of flowered chiffon, that was caught at the waist with a sash of the same material. She supposed it wasn't entirely suitable to the occasion, but she enjoyed changing into something feminine after wearing trousers for most of the day.

'I'm not cold,' she said now, and after a moment's silent appraisal he shrugged and said: 'As you like.'

He himself was dressed in the moleskin pants and silk shirt he invariably wore in the evenings, the collar unfastened to reveal the brown column of his throat. Sometimes, sitting opposite him at the table, Alexandra liked to remember what he had looked like without his shirt. He had such a nice body, she decided, wishing she understood this urge she felt to touch him all the time. He didn't invite it; he didn't even like it; but that didn't prevent her from feeling the temptation.

Outside, it was cooler than she had expected, but she wouldn't have dreamed of admitting it. It was such an unexpected treat, being alone with him like this, and she could not take the chance that if she asked him to wait while she collected a wrap, Miss Holland or Estelita might appear and decide to join them.

They crossed the courtyard at the front of the *hacienda*, and turned along the side of the house towards the paddocks. The fragrance of honeysuckle and night-scented stocks drifted to their nostrils, mingling with the earthier aromas of the animals, and the smell of roasting meat. From the bunkhouse they could hear the sound of someone playing a guitar, and more shrilly a mouth organ added its poignant harmony. The breeze that chased the clouds across the moon's curved face blew Alexandra's hair into her eyes, and she was tucking it back behind her ears when Jason turned to look at her.

'Well?' he said, and there was a trace of irony in his tones. 'I guess you have something to say to me, right?'

They had reached the poled rail of the paddock, and he turned to rest his back against the fencing, regarding her with a shadowed expression. The coolness of the breeze didn't seem to bother him, she noticed enviously, shivering a little, and deciding it was too chilly to linger, she said:

'I wanted to know why you told Ricardo not to take us into the mountains.'

Jason nodded. 'I guessed as much. Isn't it enough to know that I'd rather you remained in the valley?'

'It's not because you don't think we're capable of riding those narrow passes, is it?' she asked. 'It's something else. Is it to do with that black stallion?'

'Hell, no!' His denial was half amused, and she moved to the rail, resting her fingers over the poled surface, trying to read his expression. 'I just don't think it's a good idea, that's all. The mountains can be treacherous. When the mist comes down——'

'I'm sure Ricardo knows when the weather is likely to be dangerous,' asserted Alexandra flatly. 'Jason . . .' She turned to him appealingly, unable to resist the temptation to touch his sleeve. 'Can't you tell me the truth? I'm not a child, even though you like to treat me as one.'

Jason sighed. 'Perhaps I find it easier that way,' he remarked obscurely, and then, at her wide-eyed enquiry, he added: 'I've never had a daughter before. I'm not really equipped to deal with one.'

Alexandra pursed her lips. 'I'm not your daughter,' she declared impatiently. Then, tracing the line of the scar that was darkly visible beneath the fine silk of his shirt, she murmured: 'I see this is healing. You don't need a bandage on it any more.'

'No.' Jason was abrupt, his fingers as usual going to remove hers from their probing. 'Don't do that. I thought you came out here to find out why I wouldn't let you ride into the mountains?'

'You said you'd told me,' she reminded him softly, her fingers curving round his as he made to remove them. 'Mmm, your hands have callouses. Are they painful?'

'They're a man's hands,' he retorted. 'Working hands. Not the hands of an academic, like your father.'

'But you're that, too,' she protested, looking up at him. 'Ricardo told us. You were an engineer. He said you installed the water pipes at the house yourself.'

'Ricardo talks too much,' he stated harshly, but when her free hand came to join the other, he covered them both with his hard fingers. He stood for a long moment, looking down at their clasped hands, and then he smoothed his fingers over her knuckles. 'No one could accuse these hands of being hard, could they?' he murmured wryly. 'They're soft, as a woman's hands should be. Soft, and . . .' he raised them to his lips, '. . . sweet-smelling.'

Her heart was pounding heavily in her ears, the blood surging thickly through her veins as he spoke. The touch of those mocking lips against her skin was like a lick of flame to senses already scorched by his nearness. A feverish excitement gripped her, and although she knew she was courting danger, she did not retreat as she had done before. The feelings he was arousing inside her had to have some meaning, and in spite of her panic, she was eager to learn the truth about herself.

In the moonlight, the expression in those dark eyes was masked as he looked down at her, but presently irritation caused him to tighten his lips. 'What do you think you're doing, Alexandra?' he demanded, still gripping her fingers so tightly, she thought they might snap. 'Coming out here in that thin dress, when I can feel from your hands that you're shivering? Why did you really come? Why do you persist in running after me? Demanding attention! Encouraging me to kiss your fingers like the knight in shining armour you think I am! I'm not your *parfait* knight, Alexandra, I'm me! Just a man. Human, with all a man's weaknesses and imperfections.'

Alexandra's lips trembled. 'I know that,' she said. 'Why are you getting angry? Can't I show friendship towards you? Are you so immune from emotion that my feelings embarrass you?'

'Your feelings!' he echoed grimly. 'What feelings? What possible emotion can I arouse in your breast?'

'Affection,' she exclaimed at once. 'I'm very fond of you. You—you've been very kind to me.'

'Have I?' His tone was ironic, but she ignored it.

'Yes,' she insisted. 'And—I appreciate it.'

'Oh, I see.' His lips thinned. 'And this—this charade is in the nature of showing your appreciation, is it? There's a name for what you're doing, Alexandra, but it isn't *affection*!'

Alexandra tore her hands out of his grasp and faced him defiantly, hiding the pain he was unknowingly inflicting.

'You won't try to understand, will you?' she cried. 'All my life I've been surrounded by people who didn't try to understand how I felt, but when I met you, I stupidly imagined you might be different. But you're not. You're not! You're just as cold and unfeeling as the rest of them!'

Trembling uncontrollably now, she turned her back on him, gripping the rail with desperate fingers, needing its support as she fought back the tears that threatened to humiliate her completely. He was a brute and a bully, tying her immature overtures into knots and tearing them apart again, without either patience or sensitivity.

Wrapped up in her own misery as she was, she had not considered how Jason himself might be affected by her outburst, but even as she took little gasping breaths, trying to control her emotions, his hands closed on her arms just below her shoulders. His touch was sure and restrained, although his fingers bit into her flesh with careless strength.

'What do you know about me?' he demanded in low furious tones. 'What do you know about feelings—and emotions?' He uttered an ugly oath, compelling her backwards as he spoke, causing her to stumble against the hard, unyielding length of his body. 'You talk about friendship and affection, but what you really want is experience! Yes, *experience*!' This as she fought impotently to free herself. His arms slid around her, compressing her arms against her sides, hauling her close to the taut muscles of his lower chest and thighs. 'I knew I shouldn't have brought you here. I knew you were ripe for the kind of relationship you'd get from a boy of your own age. But you were so adamant it was what you wanted, so sure you wouldn't get bored with the limitations of our life out here——'

'I'm *not* bored!'

She almost shouted the words in her frustration, bringing up her hands to grip his arms and force him to release her. She had forgotten the vulnerable laceration in his flesh, but his uncontrollable reaction reminded her, and her anger fled in the face of his pain. Closing her eyes, she rested her head back against his chest, knowing an almost overwhelming desire to remain there, and the errant breeze whipped her hair into his face.

'Alexandra . . .' He spoke raggedly, then with a groan he bent his head and she felt the probing caress of his lips against her neck.

Almost immediately, she started to struggle, but he was stronger than she was, and in spite of his injury he overcame her futile efforts easily. Besides, as his mouth sought the hollow behind her ear, and moved exploringly along the curve of her cheek, her breathing began to quicken and other emotions weakened her desire to escape. Almost instinctively, she knew what her struggles were doing to him, and the thrusting masculinity of his body filled her with a strange and heady power. In spite of all his protests, she was capable of arousing him, and what was more, she was doing it against his will.

As he sensed her weakening, Jason's arms relaxed, and her breath caught in her throat as his hands moved upward, over her ribcage, to the pointed fullness of her small breasts. Again that sense of panic rose inside her. He ought not to be touching her there, she thought drymouthed, even while warring sensations welcomed his caress and caused her breasts to swell beneath his questing fingers.

'Don't hate me, Alexandra,' he breathed as her clenched fists brushed his thighs, but then he twisted her round to face him and his mouth on hers destroyed every shred of opposition she might have raised against him.

His mouth was firm and possessive, coaxing her lips to part and share their moist secret. Never having tasted a man's kiss before, Alexandra found herself responding blindly, unaware that her eagerness not to appear naïve made her response that much more provocative. Almost involuntarily, her hands unclenched and sought the silk-covered expanse of his chest, sliding over the fine material to touch his neck. As her arms lifted, the sleeves of her dress fell back so that skin encountered skin at her first tentative embrace. His mouth continued to explore hers, probing ever more deeply with each succeeding caress until her fingers closed on his nape, threading through the strong virile length of his hair and making their own experimental exploration.

His mouth hardened into passion and she felt as if she was drowning in sensual feeling, incoherent with emotion, scarcely conscious of the precipice she was walking. She wanted him to go on and on, uncaring of the strain she was putting on him, only wanting him to go on holding her and kissing her—letting her learn the throbbing contours of his body.

Jason finally summoned the strength to propel her away from him, but she uttered small sounds of protest, and he had to shake her half angrily to bring her to her senses. Forcing her back against the bar behind her, he kept her determinedly at arms' length, though there was compassion as well as impatience in his voice as he said:

'Well? Are you satisfied now?'

Alexandra licked her dry lips. 'Wh-why do you ask that?'

'It was what you wanted, wasn't it?' he demanded. 'Proof that you're growing into a desirable female? That even I am not totally immune to that fact, no matter how reckless proving it might be!'

She moved her slim-shoulders, realising suddenly how cold the wind had become, although she had not felt it until that moment. 'We—we're just a man and—and a woman,' she declared. 'What we just shared was the natural——'

'No!' he interrupted her curtly. 'What we just shared was not natural at all. And we're not a man and a woman. I'm a man—but you're just a provocative child who enjoys teasing!'

Alexandra gasped. 'I was not teasing!'

'What would you call it, then?'

'I've just told you.' She wrenched her arms free of him, facing him defensively. 'You're not going to pretend you didn't—didn't *want* to touch me?'

Jason stared at her for a moment, then a look of wry self-derision crossed his face and he nodded. 'Oh, I wanted to touch you, all right,' he agreed harshly. 'I wanted to do a lot more than that!'

'Did you?' Her defiance melted before the uncertainty she saw in his face. 'Did you, Jason?' Her lips parted. 'Tell me . . .'

'No!' As if regretting his momentary candour, Jason's expression hardened. 'My God, you'd like that, wouldn't you? A man of my age—and a girl obsessed with curiosity about the opposite sex!'

'That's not true!' Alexandra was hurt. 'You know it's not. I—I'm not interested in Pepe—or Ricardo, or any of the men, for that matter.'

'So what are you suggesting?' His eyes narrowed. 'That you are—interested in me?'

Her cheeks flushed. 'Is that so surprising?'

'*God!*'

'Why should you say that?' She sniffed. 'You must know how I feel about——'

He swore angrily. 'Alexandra, I'm old enough to be your father!'

'You're not!'

'I'm thirty-six. Easily old enough, believe me!'

Her lips trembled. 'I don't care how old you are.'

'No?' His mouth tightened. 'I do. And whatever fantasy you're living out so far as you and I are concerned, forget it!' He raked his knuckles down his face in sudden frustration. 'Alexandra, stop fooling yourself. What you're looking for is experience. Just that—experience. And I happened to be around to experiment on——'

'No——'

'Yes. God, I should have had more sense, I know that. But I guess I was—well, flattered that you should seek my company.'

'I don't believe that!'

'Alexandra, I don't get involved with teenagers———'

'I'm not asking you to get involved!'

'—and I make no commitments———'

'I'm not expecting you to.'

'Then what are you saying?'

Alexandra tried to remain calm. 'I—why can't we talk about it? You wanted to—to kiss me. I wanted it, too. What's wrong with that?'

'Alexandra!' With a groan of impatience, he imprisoned her within the span of his arms, resting one hand on the bole of the fence at either side of her. Then he exclaimed: 'Stop pretending, can't you? You're no sophisticate, and we both know it. I doubt if anyone's ever touched you before, have they? I shouldn't have touched you, and we both know that, too.' He paused, and she forced her gaze not to waver before the disturbing penetration of his. 'So—don't go reading anything into it that wasn't there.'

Her lips trembled. 'Thank you,' she said inexplicably, and now his eyes narrowed.

'For what?' he demanded harshly, and she lifted her chin.

'For making your position so clear,' she replied stiffly, and his knuckles showed white through his skin where his hands gripped the rail.

'You don't make it easy for me, do you?' he grated, but Alexandra only bent her head.

'Why should I make it easy for you to avoid me?' she asked, a trifle wistfully, and almost against his will, his hands left the fence to grip her waist, jerking her roughly towards him.

This time his mouth was hard and seeking, his hands intimate on her buttocks, holding her deliberately against him and letting her feel every throbbing muscle between his thighs. But if he had expected her to fight him, he was mistaken. She was still aroused and eager for his caresses, her arms around his waist sliding beneath the silk material of his shirt to probe the smooth skin of his back. Her mouth was sweet and softly parted, a cushion to the bruising pressure of his. She no longer wondered why the sheik's fair captive had succumbed to her lover's embrace. In Jason's arms, she was learning the meaning of her own destiny, the demands of her own body that instinct alone told her only Jason could assuage.

Yet, even while she luxuriated in the urgency of his ardour, she knew that Jason himself would not forgive her for what she was doing. By deliberately arousing his passion, she was slamming doors on the kind of relationship they might have had, and while she wanted him to hold her and kiss her, she didn't want him to do it against his will. That wasn't the way. Her instincts told her that, too. And for that reason, and that reason alone, she tore herself away from him to stand trembling and breathless before him.

But it was already too late; she saw that from his face. The mocking expression she had come to know so well was twisting his lips, and derision coloured his tones as he said: 'Game over? I thought so. You haven't the guts to see it through, have you? At the first sign of danger, you run for cover!'

'That's not why I——'

Alexandra broke off abruptly when she saw the cold scepticism in his face. What was the point of arguing with him? He would never believe her. And why should he?—when she hardly understood what was happening herself.

Instead, she half turned away from him—away from the sensual temptation of his lean body, that was still arousing the most disturbing sensations inside her, away from the bitter scorn in his expression, away from the agonising knowledge that her life would never be the same again. She stared blindly down at the toes of her shoes just visible below the hem of her gown, and realised she was shivering quite openly now, though she hardly felt the cold. But, as if suddenly realising this fact himself, Jason seemed to pull himself together. Thrusting his shirt back into his pants, he gripped her arm without emotion and urged her roughly towards the house.

Shaking away the sense of unreality that was enveloping her, Alexandra made one last attempt to appeal to him. 'Will—will you tell Estelita about—about this?' she demanded as he strode bleakly at her side, and then winced at the crushing contempt he turned on her.

'Oh, yes,' he answered cuttingly. 'Of course, I'll tell everyone. How shall I put it? That our youngest house guest has ideas above her—er—abilities? That my—*ward* —has an intense curiosity about matters of a wholly immoral nature? Yes. That should arouse a suitable cry of outrage among the more religious members of my household!'

'You wouldn't!' Alexandra halted, staring at him in horror, and as if relenting, his hard features took on a mocking expression.

'No,' he agreed, after a heart-stopping moment. 'No, I wouldn't.' He made a sound of impatience. 'I'm not proud of what I just did. So why should I advertise the fact?'

'Jason . . .'

'Inside!' he ordered, not prepared to discuss the matter any further, and with a heavy sigh, she preceded him into the house.

CHAPTER SIX

ALEXANDRA spent the next few days in bed.

The morning following that traumatic encounter with Jason, she awakened with a streaming head and violent pains in her stomach. Miss Holland who came to find out why she had not joined them for breakfast immediately diagnosed gastric 'flu, and insisted she would have Mr Tarrant send for a doctor.

'Oh, please, that's not necessary,' Alexandra protested weakly, trying to get up on her pillows, but Miss Holland was adamant, pressing her back with firm fingers.

'One can't be too careful in a foreign country,' she insisted. 'We can't be absolutely sure it's a form of influenza. It could be food poisoning—or pneumonia!'

Alexandra expelled her breath on a sigh. 'It's a cold, that's all, Miss Holland,' she choked, as a bout of coughing gripped her. 'Just get me some aspirin and a hot drink, and I'll stay in bed for the rest of the day. I'll be fine tomorrow . . .'

But Miss Holland was not to be thwarted, and when she returned some fifteen minutes later, Estelita was with her.

The housekeeper viewed the patient with less sympathy. Alexandra had not forgotten the look Estelita had bestowed on her the night before when she and Jason came into the house together. The housekeeper had been in the hall when they entered the *hacienda*, and Alexandra had not been able to hide the guilty flush that stained her cheeks at the woman's speculative appraisal. She had almost felt that Estelita knew exactly what had been going on, and blamed her for it, and her fingers had probed nervously at the neckline of her gown, as if she expected to find the marks of Jason's fingers there for all to see. But there was nothing

to betray her, she had reassured herself, even while that
malevolent black stare had cooled her already chilled blood.

This morning Estelita's expression was less easy to read.
There was speculation, certainly, but it was combined with
a contemptuous amusement that made Alexandra wonder
exactly what Jason had said to her. Indeed, she thought
bitterly, if she had had anything to eat or drink after returning to the house, she might have been inclined to
suspect that Estelita was responsible for her present con-
dition, but after a brief word with Miss Holland, playing
chess with Ricardo in the *salón*, she had retired to her room,
exhausted both mentally and physically.

'Mr Tarrant had already left for the stockyards,' Miss
Holland was saying now, by way of an explanation. 'So I
asked Señora Vargas to come and give us her opinion.'

Alexandra made no answer, but Estelita allowed a faint
smile to curve her thin lips. 'Miss Holland tells me you have
pains—here!' she remarked, patting her own stomach.
'You have been sick?'

'No.' Alexandra shook her head, and Miss Holland took
up the tale again.

'I think she should see a doctor,' she declared. 'It could
be food poisoning, and that can be a serious illness.'

'I have a cold!' exclaimed Alexandra futilely, as Estelita
began to protest with characteristic vehemence that her
food could not have poisoned anybody, and Miss Holland
retaliated by stating that in her opinion any highly-spiced
food was hard to digest.

It was a heated exchange which might have continued in-
definitely if Alexandra had not found it necessary to go at
once to the bathroom, and by the time she returned, weak
and trembling from an attack of vomiting, only Miss Holland remained.

'I've told Señora Vargas that I intend to get a doctor,'
she declared firmly, tucking the sheet around Alexandra's
shaking body, and the girl was too weak to argue any
further.

In the event, it was Jason who brought the doctor to San Gabriel. With her own brand of determination Miss Holland had ridden out to the stockyards and found her employer for herself, and although she accepted Ricardo's escort back to the *hacienda*, she had a distinct air of triumph on her return.

Alexandra didn't much care what happened. She was unable to swallow anything but the very smallest measure of warm lemonade, and lay feeling as if she would never lift her head again. Even the thin beef broth which Miss Holland braved Estelita's wrath to produce refused to remain on her stomach, and the muscles of her abdomen ached from constant retching. She felt wretched, and she was sure she looked wretched, and she told herself she was glad that Jason made no attempt to come and see her.

The doctor was a dapper little man in his late forties, who had his practice in Puerto Novo. He arrived in the late afternoon, and although Alexandra was sure he meant well, his probing fingers were like sharp needles against her sensitive flesh.

After satisfying himself that there was no sign of swelling or inflammation, he diagnosed a severe chill and a mild attack of gastritis, aggravated by the cold germs. He left a bottle of antibiotics, and instructions that Alexandra should remain in bed for the rest of the week.

'You see ...' Alexandra protested weakly, as Miss Holland came to tuck her up again after the doctor had departed. 'Just a cold. Nothing to get uptight about. And now Jason's got to drive to Puerto Novo and back again in the dark!'

'Mr Tarrant's not coming back,' retorted Miss Holland, briskly, straightening from her task. 'At least, not tonight, at any rate. He said he had some business to attend to in Puerto Novo anyway, so he's going to spend the night there, transact his business, and return tomorrow afternoon.'

'Oh!'

Predictably, this news was the last straw. Alexandra turned her face into the pillow and allowed the hot tears that had threatened all day to come, and blessed the fact that Miss Holland put her weakness down to physical causes.

By the end of the week Alexandra was up and about again. She was young and resilient, and the germ she had contracted was not strong enough to keep her confined to her bed for long. Even so, she accepted Miss Holland's direction not to stray beyond the immediate environs of the *hacienda*, and watched with some envy when her companion and the boisterous foreman of the *estancia* went riding together.

Encountering Jason at supper the first evening she was able to come downstairs for the meal was a nerve-racking experience. She had not seen him to speak to since the fateful evening at the paddocks, and she took her seat at the table with some misgivings. She wished she were more capable of hiding her feelings, particularly as Jason behaved little differently than usual. Apart from a polite enquiry at the start of the meal as to the state of her health, he made no effort to speak to her directly, and Alexandra realised, with a hollow emptiness in her stomach, that so far as he was concerned, the situation had not changed. His attitude was a deliberate demonstration of that fact; but that didn't prevent her from spending the meal casting covert glances in his direction, aware that her feelings towards him could not be so easily dismissed.

With time on her hands, Alexandra spent more energy in exploring the building. Whenever she knew Jason was out of the house, she ventured into his study where she had discovered a veritable library of books, many of them in English, and spent hours turning over the dusty tomes. She guessed some were books Jason had had when he was a student, but as well as theses on mechanical engineering and structural technology, there were also the novels of Dickens and Scott, alongside the more contemporary works of Scott Fitzgerald and Hemingway. She even found a copy of James Joyce's *Ulysses*, and spent a fascinating afternoon absorbed in its pages.

But the book that provided her with the most entertainment was a written course in speaking Spanish, and she set herself the task of learning another language. Her knowledge of French came in useful in the identification of words, and a natural aptitude for accent made even her first stumbling attempts sound plausible. She guessed Jason had used the book himself when he first came to South America, but she also realised that it was living in a Spanish-speaking country and hearing the language spoken every day that had given him the mastery he now possessed. Even so, it encouraged her to keep her ears ever alert for words she could recognise, and she was amazed at how swiftly she progressed.

One afternoon Estelita came upon her reciting a passage aloud from the book. She had heard the unusual sound of Alexandra's voice from beyond the door of Jason's study, and she burst into the room with scarcely concealed anger.

'*Qué hace usted aqui?*' she demanded, using her own tongue in her fury, and Alexandra astounded her by replying in kind.

'*Leo,*' she said proudly. '*Deseaba usted algo?*—is there something you wanted?'

Estelita schooled her features. 'Why are you using Jason's study?' she persisted, this time in English. 'Do you have his permission to read in here?'

Alexandra closed the book and rose abruptly to her feet. 'Do I need his permission?' she asked evenly. 'He's not here. I don't think he would object.' She gestured towards the books. 'I only read. I don't pry into his private affairs.'

Estelita's wide nostrils flared. 'What are you implying, *señorita?*'

'Nothing.' Alexandra was surprised at how quickly the other woman sprang to the defensive. 'I only meant——'

'I know what you meant, *señorita,*' retorted Estelita

angrily. 'You are quick with the—the smart answer, no? Is this what you say to Jason? Is this how you hope to twist him round your little finger, when I am not here to defend myself?'

'Estelita——

'No!' The housekeeper interrupted her, her eyes flicking scornfully over the Spanish textbook Alexandra was trying rather unsuccessfully to hide. 'So—you are learning our language, too? Perhaps you hope to persuade *el padrono* to let you stay here for ever, *no?*' Her laughter was harsh. 'You are a fool! Make no mistake, as soon as you are old enough, he will send you back. Where you belong!'

The housekeeper's departure left a lingering taste of bitterness in the air, and Alexandra found she no longer had the stomach for study. Instead, she replaced the book in its place, and left the room, admitting as she did so that Estelita had won that particular battle.

The weather, which had been particularly warm and sunny, broke the following day. Alexandra, who had been looking forward to accompanying Miss Holland and Ricardo on their morning ride, awoke to find her windows streaming with water, the curtains damp where the rain had seeped beneath the balcony doors.

Padding to the windows, she stared out bleakly on a hazy world, a grey colourless mist that blanketed the hills all around in a miserable curtain of moisture. She hardly recognised the sodden vines that clung tenaciously to the balcony rails, and she shivered in the draught that sifted through the cracks in the woodwork of her window.

Later, dressed in warm grey harem pants and a tie-waisted sweater, whose high, cuffed collar framed her face in amethyst-shaded lambswool, she went down to breakfast feeling particularly dejected. The day stretched ahead of her dull and unexciting, with the added deprivation of the privacy of Jason's study to complete her disenchantment.

The sight of Jason himself, still seated at the kitchen table drinking a mug of coffee, was a disturbing diversion, and more surprising yet was the litter of dirty dishes that adorned the table, and the fact that Estelita did not appear to be in evidence.

Jason glanced up at her appearance and then, as if compelled to do so, he rose to his feet, lean and powerful in leather jerkin and pants, long black boots completing his attire.

'You're up early,' he commented, with a polite inclination of his head. 'Do you want some coffee?'

'I can get it.' Alexandra hesitated, glancing round to find the pot still bubbling on the stove. Then, casually: 'Where's Estelita?'

Jason leant against the table, one foot raised to rest upon his chair, his expression brooding. 'Didn't she tell you?' And as Alexandra showed her bewilderment, he added: 'She's not here. Pepe's driven her to Valvedra. Their mother's ill.'

'Their mother?' Alexandra had not realised Estelita's mother was still alive, and she almost scalded herself with the coffee pot as she turned to stare at him.

'That's right.' Jason expelled his breath heavily. 'A message came yesterday, via the doctor in Puerto Novo. Señora Gomez has been ill for some time, apparently, but now she's been taken into hospital and she's asking for both her children.'

'I see.' Alexandra took a sip of the coffee, grimaced at its bitterness without either milk or sugar, and then said carefully: 'She never mentioned anything to me.'

'No.' Jason's foot dropped to the floor and he straightened. 'She didn't want to go, but I persuaded her she should.'

'You did?' Alexandra felt singularly stupid, but for the moment she couldn't think of anything else to say. Even so, it did cross her mind that this might have had some bearing on the way Estelita had spoken to her the previous day.

'Yes.' Now Jason moved round the table to light a cheroot with a taper from the fire. 'Naturally, she was concerned about her work here.' He inhaled deeply on the thin cigar. 'Estelita's a very conscientious housekeeper.'

'I'm sure she is.' Alexandra put down her coffee to add milk to its murky depths. 'So . . .' She tried to keep the note of exhilaration out of her voice. 'How long will she be away?'

Jason shrugged. 'Who can tell? Two or three days, a week? Who knows? It depends, I suppose, on her mother's progress.'

'Yes. Yes—naturally I hope she progresses well,' murmured Alexandra at once, but she saw the look of scepticism in his face.

'Do you?' he demanded, and she turned to shift the dirty dishes from the table to the sink in an effort to avoid a direct reply.

There was a curious satisfaction in the menial task, and as she worked Alexandra's mind was active. If Estelita was away, there was nobody to cook the food or look after the house. And without Pepe, too, she and Miss Holland would have the house to themselves while Jason and Ricardo were working.

With the dishes in the sink, Alexandra turned on the taps, then stepped back in surprise when Jason came across to turn them off again. Looking down into her indignant face, he said dryly: 'I'm sure you're dying to prove to me that you're every bit as efficient as Estelita, but that won't be necessary. Chan is going to cook our meals along with the others, and Andrés' wife and daughters are only too eager to come and look after us.'

Alexandra's lips pursed mutinously. 'You enjoyed telling me that, didn't you?' she exclaimed. 'You knew I'd think I could make myself useful for once, but you had to go and spoil it, hadn't you?'

Jason gave her a scornful look. 'Playing house may appeal to you at the moment,' he said, 'but I don't know how long Estelita will be away, and I can't afford to turn down Andrés' offer, when in a couple of days I may have to ask his assistance again.'

Alexandra squared her shoulders. 'Who do you think looked after my father for the six months before he died?' she demanded. 'We couldn't afford servants. I even looked after the garden!'

'Very commendable,' remarked Jason brusquely, 'but that cottage in Ealing can hardly be compared with here, can it?' He tossed the end of his cheroot into the blaze on the hearth. 'Besides, I have Miss Holland to consider.'

'She doesn't like Estelita any more than I do,' retorted Alexandra recklessly, throwing all caution to the winds. 'I should think she'd be glad to help me——'

'No, Alexandra.'

'What do you mean—no? This is supposed to be my home, too.'

'No.'

'Why not?'

Jason shook his head. 'I don't intend to argue with you.'

Alexandra moved her shoulders in a defeated gesture. 'I bet *she* made you promise not to let me do anything!' she declared childishly. She looked up at him. 'What kind of hold does she have over you, anyway? Why does she always behave as if she has some divine right to be here?' She paused. 'Miss—Miss Holland thinks she's your mistress. Is she?'

Jason stared down at her for a long moment, and then the coldness in his eyes gave way to wry admiration. 'Do you realise what you're asking?' he demanded roughly. 'If any man had said that ...'

Alexandra's face suffused with colour, and unable to sustain the penetration of his gaze, she dropped her lids to stare in acute embarrassment down at her toes. With the words uttered, she was wondering how she had dared to ask such a thing herself, and she wished the floor would open up and swallow her.

It didn't, and when Jason broke the ominous silence between them, there was a controlled tautness to his tones. 'Don't imagine what happened between us gives you any right to know where and with whom I spend my nights,' he told her grimly. 'If I have slept in Estelita's bed, that's only of concern to her—and me. Do I make myself clear?'

Alexandra's nod was jerky. 'Perfectly.'

'Good.' He moved away from her. 'So—what do you intend to do with yourself today?'

'Oh, honestly . . .' She couldn't prevent the tremor that invaded her voice as she turned on him. 'You sound exactly like Miss Holland! For God's sake, why do you persist in behaving as if I was twelve years old?'

Jason's mouth turned down. 'I think we've already had this conversation, haven't we?' he reminded her. Then he turned to the window, staring out broodingly at the pouring rain. 'Damned weather! I wanted to—well, I had things to do.'

He broke off at that point, and Alexandra, waiting for him to continue, realised that yet again she was being discriminated against. But Jason was already reaching for the thick plastic raincape that hung behind the door, and the matching leggings that went with it.

'Are—are you going out?' she asked unnecessarily, and he gave her an impatient stare.

'Does it look like it?'

'Yes.'

'Then I must be, mustn't I?'

'Are you going riding? Can I come with you?'

'In this weather? I think not.'

Alexandra hunched her shoulders. 'I can get wrapped up.'

'Look . . .' Jason was terse. 'You're just recovering from a chill. I'd be worse than mad to take you riding in conditions like these.'

'You won't let me do anything else!' she retorted sulkily, and he heaved a sigh.

'You make it very hard, Alexandra!'

'I'm sorry.'

'Oh, *God*!' He straightened after pulling on the leggings and stared resignedly at her. 'All right, all right,' he said at last. 'You can take charge of the house while Estelita's away. Does that satis——'

But he didn't finish what he had begun to say. Alexandra launched herself upon him, hugging him impulsively and bestowing an eager kiss upon his parted lips.

Maybe because he was more concerned with keeping his balance than controlling his response, Jason didn't immediately draw back from her warm mouth, and what began as a brief caress lengthened into an urgent assault on his senses. The hands that had moved to hold her back from him were suddenly gripping her closer, sliding beneath her sweater to find the soft skin of her midriff.

He tore himself away from her only as the back door burst open to admit Ricardo, but the look that accompanied his withdrawal was grim and frustrated. Avoiding his censure, Alexandra pulled her sweater down over her hips and faced the foreman's speculative gaze with all the composure she could muster.

Ricardo was followed into the room by two bedraggled girls, each holding a shawl over her head for protection, their full skirts dampened by the dash from the Range-Rover to the house. Their presence prevented him from making any comment about the scene he had interrupted, but his dark eyes were full of roguish conjecture. Alexandra guessed he would say something when he had the opportunity, but she prayed he would not chide Jason about her youth. What did it matter how old she was? When Jason held her in his arms, when he pressed her close against his lean hard body, she felt as old as Eve—and as eager to taste the forbidden fruit.

'This is Luisa and Elena Alberoni,' Ricardo was saying now, by way of an introduction for Alexandra's benefit, and she managed a faint smile in their direction. They were very alike, small and plump and dark, with their father's teak-coloured features, but the furtive glances they cast towards her spoke of shyness, not hostility. They looked at Jason shyly, too, but Alexandra recognised admiration as well as timidity in their dark eyes when they rested on the English-man.

Then Ricardo turned to his employer, who was pulling on the heavy cape he had taken down earlier. 'I told Lucia I'd fetch her if she was needed,' he explained, flicking a look at Alexandra, and although Jason faced him calmly enough, she sensed the challenge in Ricardo's words.

'My—er—Señorita Durham will tell you what she wants you to do,' Jason said now, turning to the two girls, who had taken off their shawls and were presently smoothing their curly dark hair. 'You understand a little English, don't you?'

'*Hablo un poco español*,' murmured Alexandra cautiously. 'I speak a little Spanish, too, Jason,' she added, and this time his stare held only interrogation.

'You—speak—Spanish?' he echoed. Then: 'Who taught you?'

'I taught myself,' she answered defensively, and he shook his head as if he hardly believed her.

'Well . . .' He turned to the Alberoni girls. 'You may be able to work something out.' Then, as if compelled by a force stronger than himself, he looked back at Alexandra. 'Have you been reading my books?'

She nodded. 'Some of them.'

'So it was you.' He made an impatient gesture. Then: 'You think you can cope?'

'I can try,' she responded, holding his troubled gaze, and saw with trembling delight the kindling of reluctant admira-tion in his eyes.

'Right,' he said.

'Right,' she answered softly.

But as if he suddenly realised their exchange was being closely monitored by three independent pairs of eyes, Jason walked abruptly towards the door. 'Okay,' he said shortly. 'Coming, Ricardo?' and the burly foreman paused only long enough to bestow a wicked wink in Alexandra's direction before accompanying him outside.

With the departure of the two men, the girls broke into excited whispers, and it took all Alexandra's composure to remain where she was until they chose to look in her direction again.

'*Está bien*, shall we begin?' she suggested. 'Now, you are Luisa—and you are Elena, *si?*'

'*Si.*' The elder of the two girls, Luisa, spoke. 'And you are Señorita Derem?'

'Dur-ham, actually,' amended Alexandra, with a smile. 'But you can call me Alex, yes?'

'A-lex,' said the younger girl, who Alexandra guessed was about her own age. '*Si*, Alex.'

With the matter of identification behind her, Alexandra faced her two employees with some misgivings. Pressing her palms to cheeks grown warm as much from embarrassment as from the heat from the fire, she realised she hadn't the faintest idea about what wanted doing and what didn't. In truth, she wasn't altogether sure where Estelita kept her cooking utensils or cleaning equipment, and she would have welcomed a day on her own to familiarise herself with such things. However, if she could keep the girls busy for the morning, she could spend the afternoon finding out where everything was.

Luisa and Elena were washing the dirty breakfast dishes when Miss Holland appeared. That lady came into the room like a breath of English air in the overheated kitchen, and her first action was to throw wide the window and let some of the stale air out. That it also allowed the chilly gusts

of wind to reverse the drawing power of the chimney was
soon apparent, and closing the window again, Alexandra
said:

'Estelita's gone away for a few days, so I'm in charge.'
She raised her eyebrows. 'Can I get you some breakfast?'

Miss Holland regarded the two girls who were eyeing her
with scarcely-concealed nervousness, and then said briskly:
'I'm quite capable of preparing my own breakfast, Alexandra.' She collected a cup from the dresser and approached
the coffee pot. 'Where has Señora Vargas gone?'

'To Valvedra, actually,' said Alexandra, pushing up her
sleeves and then pulling them down again, as nervous in her
own way as the other girls. 'I—er—I persuaded Jason that
I was—quite capable of running the *hacienda* in her
absence.'

'I see.' Miss Holland looked up from her coffee, which
she obviously found more palatable than Alexandra had
done. 'And can you?' she asked.

Her question took Alexandra by surprise, but she had to
admit, with characteristic candour, that she wasn't absolutely certain. 'It's finding things,' she offered, moving her
shoulders in a gesture of uncertainty. 'Estelita would never
show me where anything was kept, and when—when these
girls finish the washing up, I don't know what I'm going to
give them to do.'

'They can make the beds,' declared Miss Holland practically. 'They must know how to do that. And while they do,
we'll examine the contents of those cupboards over there.'

Adjoining the kitchen, Alexandra discovered an enormous
storeroom, and it was here Estelita kept most of the things
they needed. Sacks of rice and grain, cardboard boxes full
of tinned food, freezers crammed with meat and vegetables;
Alexandra was amazed at the variety of food there was,
and she determined that while Estelita was away they
would have a more exciting diet than the staple one of
stews and casseroles the housekeeper invariably produced.
She would speak to Chan, tell him that she intended to

cook their meals, and let Jason discover the difference for himself. She pictured them together eating candlelit dinners which she had prepared. It was a tantalising prospect and one which carried her through the exhausting day that followed.

It turned out that Estelita was not as efficient as she would have people believe. For one thing, she was not methodical, and Miss Holland, garbed in one of the house-keeper's aprons, expressed her disgust at the way many items of kitchen equipment had been allowed to tarnish. Discovering some polish, she and the Alberoni girls spent the remainder of the morning cleaning pans and cooking utensils, transforming blackened exteriors to gleaming copper and chrome.

Alexandra, cleaning out cupboards that did not look as if they had been touched for years, soon had to go and change her sweater for a cotton vest, and her face was smudged and streaked with sweat by the time Chan appeared with their lunch.

'Oh, Chan,' Alexandra exclaimed, as the cook set the dish of chili on the table, 'I wanted to speak to you. I believe Mr Tarrant asked you to prepare all our meals. Well——' she cast a defensive look in Miss Holland's direction, 'I—er—I shall be making our meals in future, so there's—er—no need for you to take the trouble . . .'

'It's no trouble,' Chan assured her doubtfully. 'You mean, you don't want supper this evening?'

'No.' Alexandra assumed a confident smile. 'I'm—er—I'm going to give Mr Tarrant some English cooking for a change. You don't mind, do you?'

Chan's smile was wry. 'It's your decision, *señorita*. I wish you luck.'

'Thank you.'

Alexandra closed the door behind him and surveyed her audience with a certain amount of defensive bravado, before she set about serving the undoubtedly expertly-cooked chili.

The rain stopped in the early afternoon, though it was still very humid, and Miss Holland supervised Luisa and Elena as they shook out rugs from the downstairs rooms, and dusted and polished the furniture. Gathering great bunches of poppies and verbena to fill the vases in the hall, Alexandra really felt as if she was making some progress, though by the time it came to start preparing the evening meal, she realised she was aching with tiredness. Perhaps she should have had Chan prepare the meal just for this one night, she thought with hindsight, but it was too late now, and Miss Holland had retired to take a bath after Andrés had arrived to take his daughters home.

She had decided to make a traditional English supper of roast beef and Yorkshire pudding, followed by baked apples and cream, but her misgivings about the meal were magnified by having to use the wood-burning stove. It was difficult deciding exactly how hot the oven was, the thermostat reading fluctuating rather erratically, but Estelita had managed and so would she.

Choosing a joint of meat was also a problem, and she wished Miss Holland was around to help her. But beef was beef, she thought, impatient with her own uncertainty, and the piece she chose looked succulent enough.

With the delicious smell of roasting meat pervading the atmosphere, she relaxed. Everything was under control. The meat was cooking; the batter for the Yorkshire puddings was made, and she had prepared the vegetables ready for boiling. There was nothing left for her to do but lay the table in the dining room, and go and change before the final preparations needed to be completed.

Miss Holland was still in the bathroom, so Alexandra went into her room and sank down wearily on to the side of her bed. Lord, she was tired! she thought exhaustedly. Even at the convent she had never worked as hard as she had worked today, and her weakness was such that she was forced to acknowledge the truth of Jason's words when he had said she was still recovering from her illness.

Flopping back against the coverlet, she allowed the softness of the mattress to mould itself to her aching bones, luxuriating in its yielding comfort. Was it really only eleven hours since she had woken in this bed? she wondered disbelievingly. It seemed much longer than that. Indeed, so much had happened since she got up that morning, it seemed more like days than hours since she had lifted her head from the pillows.

What a day! She stretched her arms lazily above her head. Starting so disastrously with the rain, and then transformed miraculously by Jason's presence. Remembering Jason, she allowed her tongue to emerge and moisten her upper lip. *Jason*, she breathed softly. Those moments in the kitchen had sustained her throughout the day. The searching pressure of his mouth, the hard muscularity of his body . . . No matter that he grew impatient with her. He couldn't deny that he enjoyed touching her, and sooner or later he would have to admit it.

A smile lifted the corners of her lips as her eyes closed, and almost before she was aware of it, sleep overtook her.

CHAPTER SEVEN

SHE awakened to a darkened room and the awareness of her near-naked body beneath the sheet. A tentative exploration essayed the knowledge that she was naked, apart from the bikini panties she wore, and her brows drew together in a concentrated effort to remember where she was and why she should be sleeping in her underwear.

The sudden crash of thunder that followed the ragged trail of lightning across the ceiling brought her upright with a start, and she stared bewilderedly towards the uncurtained windows. The storm must have awakened her, she realised uneasily, drawing the sheet about her as the cool air chilled her warm flesh. The rain was lashing against the balcony and running in rivulets down the windows, and the thunder continued to rumble round the valley, trapped by the impenetrable range of mountains.

Blinking, Alex pushed back the tangled weight of her hair and tried to think. What time was it? What time had the storm started? What time had she come to bed? And why hadn't she put on her nightgown as usual? Then she remembered . . .

Dry-mouthed, she recalled the events of the previous day —her argument with Jason and his subsequent relenting, the energy she had expended cleaning out the cupboards, and her plans for the evening that was to follow. Her *supper*!

Uncaring of the cold now, she thrust the sheet aside and put her feet to the floor. The rug was soft beneath her bare toes, and she paused a moment to wonder who had undressed her and put her beneath the covers. She guessed it must have been Miss Holland, although she was surprised she had not attempted to put on her nightgown.

Still, she had obviously not wanted to disturb her, and a sound of pure frustration escaped her. If only she had! Surely she had known how eager Alexandra was to prepare her first meal at the *hacienda*, and now that small triumph had been denied her.

Groping about in the darkness, she found her cotton dressing gown and pushed her arms into the sleeves. Then, wrapping its folds about her, she reached for the lamp. The switch clicked uselessly, and with a sigh she guessed that the storm had also fused the generating system. Making her way to the window, she peered at her wristwatch. It appeared to be after midnight, which would account for the hollow emptiness inside her, and she hunched her shoulders in despair. The evening was over. Everyone would be in bed by now. And she had not shared any of it!

Feeling ridiculously near to tears, she opened her door and peered out. Another flash of lightning illuminated the passage outside, but there was no sound other than the thunder. As she suspected, the household had retired, and only the lingering scent of her roast drifted irresistibly to her nostrils. It reminded her again that she was hungry, and with a dejected shrug she went silently along the passage to the landing.

The storm was almost directly overhead now, but she was not alarmed. Storms had never frightened her, and she was glad of the frequent discharges of electricity to light her way. Nevertheless, the resounding rumble of the thunder seemed to accentuate the isolation of their situation, and it was this that prickled goose-bumps all over her flesh as she entered the kitchen. For the first time she was glad of the log fire and the warming glow that emanated from it, and she held her hands towards the embers before helping herself to some milk from the refrigerator.

There was no sign of the joint she had roasted, she observed as she drank the milk, and another wave of resentment swept over her. Miss Holland must have made the Yorkshire puddings and served the meal herself. Had she mentioned the fact that it was she, Alexandra, who had prepared everything, who had put the joint in to roast and beaten up the batter? She sniffed. Probably the men had been so eager to eat the food they hadn't questioned its origins.

The unmistakable sound of footsteps in the yard outside dispelled all her misgivings about supper and sent a wave of apprehension tingling along her veins. Thank goodness she hadn't switched on the light, she thought weakly, wondering if it could possibly be one of the men coming home after a night on the town. Surely they didn't get prowlers out here! Not so far from civilisation.

But that was just the point, she fretted anxiously. They were so far from civilisation that laws virtually had no meaning. What kind of rough justice could anyone enforce unless with the barrel of a gun?

The footsteps seemed to be approaching the house, and in an agony of uncertainty she wondered if Jason had remembered to lock and bar the door. Was that normally Estelita's duty? Might he have forgotten it in her absence?

Almost petrified with fright, she fastened her eyes on the shadowy handle, just visible in the light from the fire. She was holding her empty glass as if it was some kind of projectile she might hurl at a possible intruder, and when the handle was depressed and the door opened inward, she nearly let it go. But even in the half-light, Jason's lean frame was unmistakable, and with a strangled cry of relief she dropped the glass to splinter noisily on to the stone floor.

'God! Alexandra!'

Jason closed the door and leaned back against it weakly as she moved into the light, and it was arguable which of them had got the worse shock.

'What the hell are you doing down here?' he demanded, recovering more quickly than she had done. 'Creeping about in the dark! Couldn't you put a light on?'

Alexandra licked her dry lips. 'The lights don't work,

she exclaimed defensively, and then gulped as Jason stretched out his hand and flicked the switch. Immediately the kitchen was flooded with light, and she was uncomfortably aware of the tumbled state she was in.

'They didn't,' he agreed, turning to lock the door before removing his soaking cape. 'But I've just been to fix them.'

'At—at this time of night?' she asked, striving for composure, and he nodded.

'We have freezers, as I believe you've discovered,' he observed. 'We can't afford to allow them to defrost.'

'No,' Alexandra nodded. 'I should have realised.'

'Why should you?' Jason had hung the cape aside now and was reaching for a towel to dry his hair. 'You're not used to our ways yet. Did the storm wake you?'

'I—I think so.' Alexandra looked doubtfully at the broken glass. 'I—I'm sorry about this. But you—you startled me.'

'You did a pretty good job of that yourself,' he remarked dryly, after towelling his head thoroughly. 'Why did you come down? Were you hungry—or frightened?'

Alexandra hesitated. 'A little of both, I suppose,' she murmured evasively, aware that her anxiety was giving way to a tingling kind of excitement. She and Jason were the only people awake in the whole house, and if he thought she was frightened . . .

'We do have pretty terrifying storms here,' Jason was saying now as he removed the thick sweater he had worn over his shirt to go outside. 'And this is a——'

The epithet he used was Spanish, but Alexandra guessed it was not a complimentary one. He grinned, and she realised it was one of the few occasions when he was not on the defensive with her. Why? she wondered. Because he felt he could handle the situation? Or because he thought she was unlikely to behave recklessly if she was frightened? The latter seemed the most likely explanation, and she speculated what he might do if he could read her thoughts at that moment.

'Had—had you gone to bed?' she asked now, bending to pick up the larger pieces of glass, and he nodded.

'I was reading,' he explained. 'It's happened before, and I was half expecting it.'

Alexandra placed the broken glass into the waste bin. Then she ventured quietly: 'I—er—I was sorry I missed supper. Did Miss Holland look after you?'

There was silence for a few moments before Jason finally said: 'Yes, I guess you could say that.'

Alexandra quelled the urge to reveal her indignation, and murmured instead: 'I feel such a fool, after—after I prepared everything.'

A curious look crossed Jason's face for a moment, then he turned away to throw a couple of logs onto the glowing embers. 'Yes, well—you were tired,' he said at last. 'We decided not to disturb you.'

'Who decided?'

Alexandra couldn't prevent her resentment from showing, and Jason glanced round at her. 'I did, actually,' he admitted. 'You were flaked out. You shouldn't have tried to do so much.'

'But this place was filthy!' she protested. 'I was only doing what should have been done months ago!'

'Maybe so.' His tone was annoyingly brusque. 'But it could have been done in easier stages.'

Alexandra pursed her lips. 'Of course, I should have known. You would say that.' Her determination to remain calm was fast disintegrating. 'You don't care that the cupboards were crawling with cobwebs or that the pans you ate out of had never seen a scrubber!'

A trace of amusement touched Jason's mouth at this point which infuriated her even more. 'I eat from plates and dishes,' he corrected her wryly, 'not pans. But do I take it you're the scrubber they've now seen?'

'Why, you—you——'

She glared at him furiously, and he relented, laughing at

her outraged face. 'I'm sorry,' he apologised. 'And naturally I do appreciate what you've done. But you shouldn't have exhausted yourself to the extent that you couldn't keep awake.'

Alexandra sniffed. 'Miss Holland should have wakened me. I wanted to serve your supper. I wanted you to enjoy a proper English meal.'

Jason shrugged, avoiding her eyes, sweeping the remains of broken glass into the hearth with his boot. 'Forget it,' he said. 'It's time we were both in bed. It's going to be a long day tomorrow.'

Alexandra was obliged to precede him up the stairs, but she dragged her feet. It was always the same. He could always better her when it came to an argument. It was only when she was physically close to him that she could weaken his resistance.

At her bedroom door, he went ahead and switched on the bedside lamp for her, standing aside as she came into the room.

'All right now?' he asked, and only then did she sense his sudden reserve.

Then, as if to deny the truth of his query, a particularly loud crack of thunder chose that moment to break over their heads, and in spite of her indifference to the storm, Alexandra started violently.

Afterwards, she wondered if her involuntary reaction had been wholly unintentional, or whether some sixth sense had known that Jason would not be immune to her fears. Whatever, the shocked pallor of her cheeks was enough to halt him in the doorway, and with a muttered curse he came back to her, throwing a reassuring arm across her shoulders.

'It's all right,' he exclaimed half impatiently, as she turned her face into the hollow below his arm. 'You're quite safe here. It sounds far worse than what it is, believe me!'

Alexandra's brain raced wildly. 'I—I hate storms,' she

lied, aware of the thudding beat of his heart beneath her cheek. 'I always have done. Ever—ever since I was a little girl.'

'You're not so big now,' muttered Jason, his breath fanning her temple. 'Shall I wake Miss Holland?'

'No!' Her response was immediate, and she lifted her head to gaze appealingly at him. 'No, don't do that. I mean—well, I'd feel such a fool . . .'

'Will you be all right on your own, then?' he asked, and she sought desperately for some means to detain him.

'Couldn't—couldn't you stay—just for a while? Until—until the storm's over?'

'Me?' Jason would have drawn away, but she caught the hand that rested on her shoulder and clung to it. 'Alexandra, the storm could go on all night!'

'Oh, please . . .'

She put such entreaty into her voice that unwillingly, he was moved, and half closing his eyes, he said: 'I can't stay here, but if you're really afraid to be alone, you'd better come along to my room.'

'To your room!'

Her voice rose an octave as she repeated his words, and she cleared her throat to disguise her sudden apprehension.

'Why not?' he countered now. 'One bedroom is much like another, and I do not intend outraging Miss Holland's sensibilities by spending the night in yours.'

Alexandra hesitated. She wasn't afraid, exactly, she told herself. It was just that she had never been in a man's company at this time of night before, and while her bedroom seemed safe and secure, his was alien territory. Then she chided herself. This was what she had wanted, wasn't it? By staying here, she would be admitting to a childish impulse to keep Miss Holland within calling distance.

'All right,' she agreed at last, and with a curt inclination of his head, Jason gestured her towards the door.

He switched out the lamp and closed her door before following her along the passage to his room. Then, as she hung back, he opened his door and urged her inside.

The thunder rumbled ominously around the house as she seated herself awkwardly in the armchair beside his bed. Jason closed the door, and avoiding his gaze, she turned her attention to the tumbled sheets. The book he had been reading was turned face-downwards on the coverlet, and from its jacket she could see it was a contemporary novel by a well-known author. But she could not summon the courage to pick it up and found her eyes focussing on a pair of cream silk pyjama trousers that were thrown carelessly across his pillow. Almost instinctively, her hands moved to touch the fine material, smoothing it between her finger-tips and gaining a certain sensuous satisfaction from the texture.

'What are you doing?'

Jason's voice from just above her alerted her to the fact that he had come to stand in front of her. He stood looking down at her, feet slightly parted, big and powerful, and devastatingly sexual—and she wanted him to touch her so badly she had a physical ache inside her.

Lifting the yielding fabric of the garment, she cradled it against her cheek and only Jason's jerking it out of her grasp prevented her from turning her lips against the soft threads. Balling the pyjamas with impatient fingers, Jason hurled them across the room, then said angrily: 'So that's why you came, is it? My God, what did they teach you in that convent of yours?'

Alexandra's face burned, but she remained where she was, even while every nerve in her body cried out for her to get to her feet. 'I—I don't know what you mean,' she protested huskily, but she could see that he didn't believe her.

'Your father would be proud to see you now, wouldn't he?' Jason continued relentlessly. 'Insinuating yourself into a man's bedroom, pretending you were afraid of the storm——'

'I said I didn't like thunder; I don't!'

'Is that your excuse for promiscuity?'

That brought her to her feet, quivering with indignation, the force of the sense of injustice she was feeling overcoming her fear of his anger: 'I'm not promiscuous!' she declared fiercely. 'Just—just because I turn to you, because —as you pointed out—I have no father, you behave as if I was some kind of—of *groupie*!'

'Oh, come on ...' He turned away, raking agitated fingers through his hair. 'You didn't come in here looking for a father figure. We both know the little games you like to play. Only it's late and I'm tired, and not altogether in control of my actions, do I make myself clear? You may find the lateness of the hour romantic, but I find it only irritating, and if you're not scared of the storm, I suggest you go back to your own room before you run into something you can't handle.'

Alexandra's throat was dry. 'You mean—you mean you'd like me to stay here?'

'God Almighty!' His ejaculation was harsh and angry. 'How you do like to talk about these things!' He turned to glare at her. 'All right, I'll lay it on the line. Right now, I'd like to sleep with you, yes. But if—Estelita was here, she would do just as well!'

'*Oh!*'

Alexandra's hand went to her mouth, in horror at the obscenity of his words. He had been cruel before, but never so brutal, and she felt as if she had received a violent slap in the face.

'So,' he continued ruthlessly, 'do we understand one another now?' and as she nodded she felt the prickling heat of tears running down her cheeks and invading the parted contours of her mouth.

'Oh, God!' As if realising he had gone too far, Jason stepped into her path as she would have rushed to the door, gripping her shoulders with biting fingers and shaking her ever so gently. 'Alexandra!' he exclaimed frustratedly. 'I'm sorry ...'

Alexandra tried to pull away from him. 'Let me go,' she cried, in a muffled voice. 'You don't have to feel sorry for me!'

'Sorry for you!' Jason continued to hold her despite her struggles. 'Hell, I think it's me I feel sorry for most!' and with a defeated sound he hauled her towards him.

With his face buried in the scented hollow of her neck, it was incredibly difficult for Alexandra to remain unmoved. She felt his lips probing the sensitive nerves at her nape, and her hands crushed between them were all too conscious of the contracting muscles of his flat stomach. But what seduced her most was the warm scent of his body, the clean male smell of him that made her want to feel him so much closer than the barrier of his clothes would permit. His mouth trailed fire along her jawline, and then found hers, one finger parting her lips and invading the moistness within.

That was when she lost all control of her actions. Winding her arms around his neck, she strained closer to him and felt the unmistakable response of his body. Her breasts surged against his chest, and without releasing her mouth, Jason unbuttoned his shirt and pushed her wrapper off her shoulders. It parted easily, and with a groan of satisfaction, he swung her off her feet and carried her to the bed.

Somehow, he had shed his clothes and the length of his body was firm and smooth along the length of hers. His lips were probing her nipples now, stroking and nuzzling their pointed fullness, driving her to dizzying heights of desire as he continued to caress her. His mouth frequently returned to the urgency of hers, and her hands were gripping the hair at his nape, holding him closer, when there was a sudden knocking at the door.

It was only then that Alexandra realised Jason had left the lamp on, painting their bodies in its golden glow of warmth and intimate isolation. But they were isolated no longer. Someone was knocking at the door, demanding

admittance, and even as Alexandra shook her head appealingly, Miss Holland's voice called:

'Mr Tarrant! Mr Tarrant! Are you there? Can I speak to
you for a moment?'

Jason went rigid, and his lids closed over the torment in
his eyes. 'No,' he muttered, 'not now ...' and Alexandra
twisted her arms around his neck.

'Don't answer,' she whispered achingly. 'She'll go away.'

'And if she doesn't?' he demanded thickly. 'No, damn
her, I've got to answer!'

Rolling away from her, he groped impatiently for the
pyjama trousers he had thrown aside earlier, sliding his
legs into their silken casing. Then, as he pulled on a towelling bathrobe, he looked down at Alexandra, still lying as he
had left her.

'Get under the covers,' he directed huskily. 'I won't be
long.'

Obediently, Alexandra scrambled into the bed, and with
a tense expression Jason went to the door. Miss Holland
was waiting outside, an anxious figure in her blue woollen
dressing gown and hairnet, her face creamed for the night.

'Oh, Mr Tarrant,' she exclaimed, as he stepped outside,
half closing the door behind him. 'I'm so worried. Alexandra's not in her room.'

Alexandra, lying listening, could well imagine Jason's
reactions to this statement, but his voice was composed as
he said: 'She's not?' in quiet tones.

'No.' Miss Holland continued: 'I was awakened—I don't
know why. I thought it might have been the storm, or
perhaps a sound from Alexandra's room. I was concerned
about her. After all, she's had nothing to eat since lunchtime. So I got out of bed and went to investigate. But she's
not there. Her bed's empty.'

There was silence for a moment, and then Jason said:
'Perhaps she's gone downstairs to get something to eat,' but
Miss Holland didn't think this was likely.

'There are no lights on,' she offered doubtfully, but Jason

seemed determined to make her believe that this was the most likely explanation.

'She probably turned them out after her,' he said shortly. 'After all, she wouldn't want to disturb anybody, would she?'

'You may be right . . .' Miss Holland was wavering now. 'Do you think I should go and see?'

Jason hesitated. Then he said: 'Maybe that would be the best thing. I wouldn't want to—well, alarm her. I'll put on some clothes while you're gone, and if she's not there, I'll go look for her.'

'But where else could she be?' fussed Miss Holland, still obviously most distressed, and Jason soothed her with reassurances that her charge must be somewhere in the house.

'She'd hardly go out on a night like this, would she?' he reasoned, and the woman was forced to concede that her anxieties were probably groundless.

But after Miss Holland had gone on her way, Jason came back into the bedroom with less composure. 'Come on,' he said, as Alexandra stared wordlessly at him. 'Out! I want you safely back in your own room before Miss Holland returns.'

'*Jason!*'

He turned away from the appeal in her wide violet eyes. 'I mean it, Alexandra. I was a fool to let you stay here. Now, hurry!'

'But, Jason——'

'Oh, God!'

He turned back then, tossing the covers aside and lifting her bodily out of the bed. But the feel of her yielding body against his was almost his undoing, and for a moment his mouth sought for hers, hard and passionate, and unutterably desperate.

'You have to go,' he groaned, even while his hands lingered on the creamy roundness of her shoulders, and she leant towards him to touch his throat with her lips.

'I love you,' she whispered, her breath mingling with the tortured expellation of his, and he had to tear himself away from the invitation in her eyes.

'Go to bed, Alexandra,' he muttered raggedly, and with a little choking sob, she left him.

Miss Holland came knocking at her door a few minutes later, raising her eyebrows in surprise when Alexandra answered, wrapped in her dressing gown.

'You were in the bathroom all the time,' she accused softly. 'Oh, my dear! I was so worried.'

'There was no need,' replied Alexandra tautly, and the other woman shook her head.

'Didn't you hear me talking to Mr Tarrant? I'm afraid I disturbed him unnecessarily.'

'Yes,' Alexandra nodded, 'he told me.'

'Oh, dear!' Miss Holland looked, if anything, even more concerned. 'He found you, of course. He seemed rather— annoyed about the whole affair. But if only I'd known . . .'

'Can we talk about this in the morning?' asked Alexandra, interrupting her. 'I—well, I am rather tired, Miss Holland . . .'

'Oh—oh, of course.' Miss Holland was apologetic, which made Alexandra feel even worse. 'Goodnight, my dear. Sleep well.'

'Thank you.'

Alexandra closed the door and leant against it for several minutes before moving to the bed. Then when she did seek the comfort of the mattress, it was only to sit staring blindly into the darkness. Jason wouldn't come now, she knew it, and she also knew that by blurting out her feelings for him she had humiliated herself completely.

CHAPTER EIGHT

THE next morning Alexandra slept in, and it was after nine o'clock before she dragged herself downstairs to find Miss Holland just taking a tray of bread rolls out of the oven. The Alberoni girls were there, too, peeling vegetables at the sink, and Alexandra felt an intruder in the kitchen.

It was a beautiful morning outside. The storm had left a certain lushness in the air, and the pasture sloping down to the river looked rich and succulent. The sun was already high, and a smell of damp warmth invaded the open door. The chickens were scratching noisily about the yard, and somewhere a blackbird was singing its heart out. It was the kind of day when it was good to be alive, but Alexandra only felt the crushing weight of depression.

She hovered awkwardly beside the scrubbed table, and Miss Holland set a mug of coffee and a plate containing a hot roll and some butter in front of her.

'Help yourself,' she offered briskly. Then: 'Luisa, when you've finished those beans, you can go and ask Chan where Mr Tarrant keeps his wine.'

Alexandra subsided into the chair beside the table, but although she sipped desultorily at the coffee, she made no attempt to touch the food. Miss Holland looked so at home in the kitchen, so calm and efficient, while she was struggling to remember the enthusiasm she had had the previous day.

With Luisa gone across the yard to speak to the Chinese cook and Elena outside, emptying the peelings, Miss Holland turned her attention to the girl hunched so dejectedly over the table.

'If I didn't know better, I'd say that Mr Tarrant had found the time to tell you what a disaster supper was last even-

115

ing,' she remarked candidly, and Alexandra was shocked
into attentiveness.

'My supper!' she gasped. 'What was wrong with it?'

Miss Holland uttered a mirthless laugh. 'What was right
with it, you mean?' She shook her head. 'My dear child, you
don't roast shoulder of beef, at least, not unless you have
several hours to spare.'

Alexandra stared at her, her own miseries forgotten in
defence of her cooking. 'Are you saying the meat was
tough?'

'A little,' commented Miss Holland dryly.

'It's that oven!' declared Alexandra at once. 'It wasn't
hot enough.'

'On the contrary, if anything it was too hot.'

Alexandra pursed her lips. 'And the Yorkshire puddings?'

'They were all right, I suppose. A bit lumpy, but that
couldn't be helped.'

Alexandra's breathing came in shallow gulps. 'What—
what did—what did they say?'

'Who? Mr Tarrant and Señor Goya?' Miss Holland
shrugged. 'They were sympathetic, I think.'

'Sympathetic!' Alexandra almost choked with frustration. 'I don't want their sympathy!'

Miss Holland shrugged again. 'I thought I ought to warn
you,' she declared evenly. 'I would have woken you last
evening, but Mr Tarrant said it was kinder to let you sleep.'

Alexandra's bubble of indignation burst. 'You mean—
you mean Jason—stopped you from waking me?'

'That's right. He went upstairs, and when he came down
again he said you'd fallen asleep.'

'Did he?' With tremulous awareness, Alexandra recalled
her eventual wakening during the storm. Tentative fingers
strayed over her breast, its pointed tip probing her palm
through the thin material of her cotton shirt, reminding her
of her nakedness. Her mouth was dry as she added: 'Did
he say anything else?'

'Not then, no.' Miss Holland poured herself a cup of

coffee, before continuing: 'What happened? Did you intend to have a nap or what?'

'No.' Alexandra shook her head vigorously. 'I just—closed my eyes. That's all I remember.'

'And then I suppose you got undressed before you went to the bathroom?'

'What?' Alexandra felt her cheeks turning pink. 'Oh—oh, yes, that's right. I—I must have disturbed you.'

'Yes.' Miss Holland sipped her coffee, viewing the girl over the rim of the cup. 'What did Mr Tarrant say when he discovered where you were?'

'N-nothing much.' Alexandra made an offhand gesture. 'Only—only that you were looking for me.'

'I see.' Miss Holland nodded slowly. Then, as if dismissing the topic, she turned back to the stove. 'Well, I suggest you go and get some air now. You're looking rather peaky. I'd join you myself, only I want to make a pie for supper. Does steak and kidney appeal to you?'

Alexandra sighed. 'I can't just go and—and leave you to it!' she protested.

'You can and you will,' insisted Miss Holland firmly. 'You've already had one dose of illness. Don't invite another. You worked hard yesterday. Today you can get some sun on those pale features.'

Ricardo came upon her as she was helping old Jave to sweep out the stables. It was cool and musty in the stables, the smell of the horses a balm to her troubled spirit. She enjoyed the exertion, too, and the comradeship she shared with the elderly Indian who understood her stumbling attempts at Spanish.

When Ricardo's huge shadow darkened the doorway, she thought for one heart-stopping moment that it was Jason come to find her. Then the foreman's hearty laugh rang out, and he exclaimed reprovingly: 'What's this? I thought the old one told me you were taking a rest, *niña*!'

Alexandra straightened, her back aching a little from the

stooped position she had been adopting. But she managed
a faint smile of greeting, and said lightly: 'I wanted to go
riding, but you weren't around to take me.'

'Ah-ha!' Ricardo tapped the side of his nose significantly
and grinned. 'But I am here now, *no*? And I have brought
someone to meet you. My son—Manuel.'

'Your son?' Alexandra followed him out into the bright
sunlight of the yard. She had heard Ricardo speak of his
son before. She knew he worked for Jason, too, but like the
other men, he seldom ventured up to the house.

She would never have recognised the young man leaning
against the bole of the gnarled old eucalyptus tree outside
as Ricardo's son. He was of a much slighter build than his
father, and his features were pale, not swarthy. His eyes
were shy, not bold like Ricardo's, and his hair was as
smooth and straight as his father's was unruly. Only his
clothes matched those of the other men—shirt, waistcoat
and pants, with leather chaps to protect his legs.

He straightened at their approach, and although his
smile was gentle and unassuming, Alexandra was immediately conscious of the state of her hands and of the fact
that her face was probably streaked with dirt, too.

'My son,' said Ricardo again, rather unnecessarily.
'Manuel, this is Señorita Durham.'

'I know.' Manuel spoke as good English as his father, if
not better, and his voice was quieter, more cultivated.

'Manuel has been working at the *estancia* since he
finished college three months ago,' stated Ricardo proudly.
'But it is only a temporary arrangement. He is going to be
an engineer—like the *patrón*!'

'What my father really means is that at present I am
unemployed,' put in Manuel, with a grimace. 'There are not
as many vacancies for engineers as there are for *gauchos*.'

Alexandra found herself smiling at him. He really was
a handsome young man, she thought approvingly, glad that
there was at least someone else besides Jason who could
disconcert Ricardo.

'And do you like being a *gaucho*?' she asked easily, and Manuel nodded.

'In summer, the work is good,' he conceded. 'Much better than some stuffy office. But come winter——'

'Come winter, you will be working in Brazil,' declared Ricardo uncompromisingly. 'You know Fredriksons have offered you a job!'

Manuel shrugged. 'I do not know that I want to go and work in Brazil,' he retorted, winking at Alexandra. 'And in any case, my plans can be of no interest to Señorita Durham.'

'Oh, they are——' Alexandra was beginning, when Ricardo interrupted her.

'It is true,' he agreed ruefully. '*Señorita*, Manuel is here to take my place for a few days, no? The *patrón* has need of me, and it was his suggestion that Manuel might be a suitable replacement. If you have no objection, *por supuesto*.'

Jason's suggestion! Alexandra felt the hot colour invading her cheeks even while a feeling of deflation filled her. Jason's suggestion that this handsome young man, should take his father's place and keep her company. Should *waste* his time escorting her! And why? Because he had no time for her? Because he wanted to keep her off his back?

On the point of telling Ricardo that she needed no one to accompany her, resentment gripped her. Why should she satisfy Jason's ego to that extent? If he thought she could find a replacement for him as easily as for Ricardo, he might lose a little of that arrogance he possessed in such abundance. And Manuel was a very handsome young man ... Handsome, *and intelligent*, she amended bitterly, and nearer her own age, if she was not mistaken.

Now she rubbed her dirty hands over the seat of her pants, and said tautly: 'That was—very kind of him—of all of you. Particularly as I'm sure Manuel has more important things to do than provide me with an escort.'

'You have to be joking!' declared that young man, with gratifying eagerness. 'I shall be happy to be at your service, *señorita*,' and his father added his assurances.

'Manuel will take good care of you,' he promised, glancing up towards the sun, climbing to its zenith. 'And don't forget to wear your hat, *no*?'

It was good to feel the chestnut's flanks beneath her once more. Leaving the *hacienda* behind, Alexandra gave the mare her head, lying low over her neck as they galloped recklessly across the turf. Manuel was hard put to keep pace with her on his sturdy animal, which was built more for stamina than for speed, and eventually Alexandra relaxed and waited for him to catch up.

'Sorry about that,' she apologised ruefully. 'But it's ages since I came out here.'

'You've been ill. My father told me,' commented Manuel, reining in his palomino beside her. 'I hope you are fully recovered now.'

'Oh, yes.' Alexandra gave a wry laugh. 'It was only a chill.'

'But serious enough to get the doctor from Puerto Novo.'

'Oh . . .' Alexandra kicked her heels into the mare's sides and the horses ambled on together. 'That was Miss Holland's idea. You haven't met Miss Holland, have you? She's my—er—companion.'

'I have seen her,' nodded Manuel humorously. 'We see her riding about the *estancia*. She wears a round hat and trousers—like this!'

He pulled the leather chaps out from his legs in imitation of Miss Holland's jodhpurs, and Alexandra smiled. 'That's right,' she assented laughingly. 'Actually, they are what people wear to go riding in England. Only hers are rather—old-fashioned.'

'Hmm.'

Manuel showed his agreement, and they rode on for some way in silence. They followed the track Alexandra

had learned with Ricardo, curving along the river for some
distance, and then climbing steadily into the foothills. The
scent of pine and juniper was strong after the rain, and the
heat of the sun sent little swirls of mist rising from the
undergrowth. Alexandra was glad of the coolness provided
by the brim of her hat, but her hand went often to push
the weight of her hair back from her brow.

If she turned sideways in the saddle, she could see the
roof of the *hacienda* below them in the valley, the river
swollen by the storm surging greedily downstream. She
could see the rainswept branches of the acacia behind the
storeroom, and the strewn petals of the blossoms that had
been devastated during the night.

Turning back to Manuel, she said suddenly: 'Do you
think we might see the black stallion today? He's a beautiful beast, isn't he? So strong and powerful! I've seen him a
couple of times already, but what I'd really like to do is get
close to him.'

'Would not we all?' Manuel replied dryly. Then, quellingly: 'I do not think it is likely, *señorita*. It is safer if we do
not ride into the gullies until the prowler has been caught.
My father said——'

But Alexandra had stopped listening to him. 'What
prowler?' she demanded tensely, and she could tell immediately from Manuel's expression that he knew he had said
the wrong thing.

'It is not important,' he protested, turning aside to point
to a flock of geese rising from the reeds beside the river.
'See the colours of their tail feathers, *señorita*. Are not
they beautiful, too? I had a friend, at the university, he
used to paint the birds——'

'Manuel!' She leant across to grip the horn of his saddle,
staring impatiently into his face. 'I'm not interested in
birds, and nor are you. I want to know what you meant by
a prowler! Do you mean there is someone—some man——'

'Man? No!' Manuel shook his head, looking down at her

fingers restlessly massaging the iron hook that he used
when he was roping cattle. 'No human prowler this,
señorita. Not at San Gabriel.'

'Then what?' Alexandra stared at him, but already an
idea was occurring to her. 'An animal of some sort?' she
questioned. 'A—a cat? A big cat?' Watching his expressive
features as she spoke, she felt sure she was on to the right
track. 'A lion?' she asked, with deepening apprehension.
'That's it, isn't it? A mountain lion?'

Manuel's shoulders sagged. 'A jaguar, most likely,' he
agreed heavily, 'and my father will have my hide for telling
you.'

'So that was why Jason——' Alexandra broke off
abruptly as she felt the first twinges of real fear. Turning
wide eyes in Manuel's direction, she exclaimed: 'But I
thought wildcats kept to their own territory. Surely they
don't venture down into the valley!'

'Not normally,' Manuel conceded. Then, as if deciding
that as she already knew the worst there was no harm in
talking about it, he sighed and went on: 'Cats are pre-
dators, but as you say, they don't usually prey near men.
However, there are exceptions to every rule, and when an
animal is old . . . or sick . . .'

Alexandra licked her dry lips. 'You mean—this animal is
one of those things?'

Manuel hesitated. 'I believe so,' he admitted at last, but
she sensed he was still holding something back.

'Have—have you seen it?' she asked, involuntarily tightening her hand on the mare's reins, but Manuel shook his
head.

'Not me, no.'

'But your father? Or Jason?'

'They may have done,' he conceded, but she was not
satisfied.

'Manuel!' she cried frustratedly. 'If you know something
else, tell me! I—I *have* to know.'

Pictures of Jason riding alone into the mountains in search of some dangerous wild animal were flooding her brain. And even while she accepted that he would not take unnecessary risks, that he would be armed, she knew now that that was what he had intended to do the previous day had the weather not prevented him.

Manuel shifted uncomfortably in his saddle as she continued to gaze at him and finally he said: '*Está bien*, she is wounded! Carlos, one of *el patrón's* men fired on her three weeks ago.'

'You're sure?'

'*Estoy seguro*,' declared Manuel, speaking Spanish in his agitation. '*El patrón* himself has seen her. Unfortunately, he did not have his rifle with him at the time.'

'Oh, *lord*!' Imagining the worst that could have happened, Alexandra moved her head in a helpless gesture. 'And—and this creature has come down into the valley?'

'After dark, yes,' said Manuel reluctantly.

'Has it killed?'

Manuel uttered a harsh sound. 'Do cats not always kill? *Si, señorita*, she has killed. Sheep—cattle—and two nights ago, a horse.'

'How awful!' Alexandra looked round at the low range of hills ahead of them with new eyes. 'And—and it's hiding somewhere in there?'

'Somewhere,' agreed Manuel flatly. 'And now, come! I think we should be turning back, *no*?'

Alexandra's lips twisted. 'Are you frightened?' she taunted, and then felt remorse as the young man showed his indignation.

'No!' he declared fiercely. 'But my father——'

'I know, I know.' Alexandra pulled an appealing face at him. 'Your father told you not to take me into the mountains. Come on, then. I'll race you back to the river.'

'Take care!' he cried anxiously, as she swung the mare's head round and dug her heels into its flanks. But Alexandra only grinned at him, finding release from her own anxieties as the breeze's errant fingers tore the sombrero from her head.

She had almost reached the river when she saw him. Closer now than ever before, the stallion stood proudly on a ridge just across the swiftly-flowing current. He seemed to be staring straight at her, although she guessed his attention was more for the mare than for its rider, but she reined in wonderingly, her lips parting at his unconscious symmetry.

Manuel thundering up behind her was caught off balance, and his mount reared protestingly as he hung on the bit. The sudden commotion startled the stallion, and with an arrogant flick of its tail, it turned and plunged away across the *pampa*.

Alexandra was unreasonably irritated by what she considered Manuel's carelessness, and his casual comment that the stallion was a nervous brute caught her on the raw.

'You should be so nervous!' she retorted, tossing her head. 'He's beautiful! The most beautiful animal I've ever seen.'

Manuel shrugged, and infuriated by his indifference, Alexandra urged the mare forward, plunging down the slope towards the river with more enthusiasm than common sense. She guessed what was about to happen almost before disaster overtook her, but that didn't prevent the mare from putting its head down so that Alexandra went hurtling head over heels into a bank of lush grass.

She wasn't really hurt, only stunned, the breath knocked out of her, but Manuel scrambling down the slope after her wore an expression of such anxiety that she was tempted to pretend she had been knocked out. However, her innate sense of fair play would not allow her to tease him in that way, particularly when she had been to blame, and his hoarse; 'Alexandra?' as he hovered over her, brought a smile of reassurance to her lips.

'I'm all right,' she said softly, and he wrenched off his hat to twist it tortuously between his fingers.

'*A Dios gracias*,' he muttered, his face as pale as hers had become, and she rolled on to her knees to stretch a hand towards him apologetically.

'You called me Alexandra,' she said, squeezing his forearm which was agreeably muscular. 'I wish you would use my name. *Señorita* is so—formal!'

Manuel closed his eyes for a moment, and then opened them again to wipe the sweat from his brow with the brim of his hat. 'I was so worried!' he confessed. 'You are sure you are not hurt?'

Alexandra withdrew her hand to spread her arms expressively. 'Do I look hurt?' she demanded, and his handsome features suffused with colour.

'No,' he conceded softly. 'You look—*muy hermosa*.'

Alexandra's lips parted. 'I know what that means.'

'Do you?' He got to his feet, holding out a hand to assist her, and as she put her hand into his she said: 'You're very gallant, particularly after what happened.'

Manuel grinned. 'A beautiful girl always deserves gallantry.' Then he added: 'The mare has gone. I think we should make haste to the stables before Jave thinks I have lost you.'

Getting to her feet, Alexandra winced a little as the sudden action reminded her she had hit her head as well as other parts of her body. She allowed Manuel to help her up the slope to where the patient palomino waited, and then said:

'I can't take your horse! That wouldn't be fair!'

'I did not intend that you should,' retorted Manuel dryly. 'Piso can carry both of us, if you permit?'

Alexandra hesitated only a moment before swinging herself up on to the palomino's back. Why not? she thought recklessly. If Jason didn't like it, he had only himself to blame. She comfortably forgot that if she hadn't lost her temper and been thrown, the situation would not have occurred.

Miss Holland was waiting by the boundary fence when they rode back to the *hacienda*. Her anxious face was evidence of the agonising few minutes she had spent, but relief quickly gave way to disapproval when she realised Alexandra was all right. She looked askance at the way her charge had been returned to her, secure within Manuel's controlling arms, and hurried the girl down from the horse as soon as they reached her.

'It was my fault,' declared Alexandra at once, as Miss Holland began to remonstrate with her escort, and smiling up at Manuel, added quickly: 'It was all my fault. I was careless—showing off! I'm sorry the mare came back alone to worry you.'

Miss Holland pursed her lips. 'Being sorry is hardly compensation for my feelings when I saw that chestnut mare!' she exclaimed. 'Dear heaven, what have you been doing? There's grass all over your hair.'

Alexandra grimaced, pulling green strands out of the silky curtain about her shoulders. 'Manuel tumbled me in the hay,' she offered wickedly, but Manuel's mortified expression more than convinced Miss Holland that she was not telling the truth.

'You can tell me what happened later,' she told the girl shortly. 'Now I suggest you go and wash for lunch, and thank your lucky stars Mr Tarrant wasn't around when your mount came back!'

Alexandra's brief moment of exhilaration fled. 'I doubt if he would have noticed,' she stated tautly, before glancing up at Manuel again. 'Will I see you tomorrow?' she asked, horrifying Miss Holland still further by her presumption, and Manuel made a helpless gesture.

'If you wish . . .' he began, and Alexandra nodded.

'I wish,' she said, and sauntered away towards the house before Miss Holland could attempt to alter the arrangement.

CHAPTER NINE

'THERE was absolutely no need to behave so recklessly,' declared Miss Holland later that day, as she and Alexandra ate lunch together. 'You could have been killed! Don't you know you could have broken your neck!'

Alexandra pushed the delicious Spanish omelette round her plate, and chewed absently on a lettuce leaf. 'I didn't fall deliberately,' she protested, unable to deny the anxiety of not knowing where Jason was or what he was doing. 'It was just an accident, that's all. It won't happen again.'

'I'm sure it won't,' Miss Holland affirmed grimly. 'In future, I shall go with you, and I shall ensure you don't do anything foolish.'

Alexandra was too distraite to argue with her. Instead, she pushed her plate aside and said: 'What range does a rifle have?'

'A rifle!'

Miss Holland was clearly taken aback, and Alexandra pressed the advantage. 'A rifle, yes,' she said. 'I want to know how near a man has to be to a lion to be sure of killing it.'

Miss Holland stared at her bewilderedly. 'Really, Alexandra, you are the most perplexing child!'

'I'm not a child!'

'All right—girl, then.' The older woman sighed. 'What has the range of a rifle to do with our conversation?'

'Jason carries a rifle,' replied Alexandra idly. 'I'm—interested, that's all.'

'Well, I'm afraid that's a question you'll have to ask him,' said Miss Holland, getting up to clear the plates. 'I know nothing about firearms. Horrible things!'

'Didn't Lord Carleon ever go shooting?'

Miss Holland frowned, obviously puzzled at this turn of the conversation. 'Well—yes,' she admitted at last. 'But that was different. He used a shotgun, not a rifle.'

Alexandra traced the grain in the wooden surface of the table with a fingernail. 'Shotguns aren't like rifles, I agree. With a rifle, you must be accurate. Shotguns spray pellets in all directions.'

'Well, I wouldn't say that,' retorted Miss Holland indignantly. 'Besides, they're two entirely different weapons.' She shook her head impatiently. 'That young man—Manuel—hasn't been filling your head with ideas of a hunting expedition, has he? Because I warn you——'

'No!' Alexandra hunched her shoulders. 'It's *el patrón* who's gone hunting!'

'*El patrón?* You mean—Mr Tarrant?'

'That's right.' Alexandra looked challengingly up at her. 'Didn't you know?'

Miss Holland made a confused gesture. 'Know? What could I know? Alexandra, what are you talking about?'

Alexandra looked down again. 'Perhaps I oughtn't to tell you,' she murmured infuriatingly. 'After all, I wasn't supposed to know myself.'

'Alexandra!'

'Oh, all right . . .' The brief stimulation she had derived from teasing the other woman quickly dissipated as the seriousness of Jason's mission swept over her again in chilling perspective. 'Some mountain lion's been raiding the *estancia*,' she admitted, the tremor in her voice belying her offhanded tones. 'Manuel told me.'

Miss Holland's reactions were less emotional than Alexandra's had been, but her lips were perceptibly tighter as she said: 'I gather he didn't have Mr Tarrant's permission to do so. He should have had more sense.'

'Why?' Alexandra was indignant. 'Why shouldn't we be told? We're not children!'

'No. But probably Mr Tarrant didn't want to alarm you

unnecessarily. I shall speak to Ricardo about that young man——'

'No! No, don't.' Alexandra sprang to her feet. 'He didn't mean to tell me. It—it was just something he said. It slipped out.'

'Nevertheless, he should be taught to guard his tongue.'

Alexandra sighed. 'Oh, honestly . . .' She moved restlessly towards the windows. 'What does it matter? It's Jason who's out there looking for the creature, not us. We're safe enough, aren't we?'

Miss Holland shrugged and moved to lift the coffee pot from the stove. 'I don't think you have any need to worry about Mr Tarrant, if that's what you're implying.'

'Don't you?' Alexandra's throat was dry.

'No.' Miss Holland was brusque. 'Now, I suggest you come and finish your lunch. As I've sent Luisa and Elena home, I shall want your help with the washing up.'

Alexandra was in her room when Jason and Ricardo returned. She heard their voices in the hall, and her heart beat a little faster with the relief of knowing that they were unharmed. She wondered if they had caught the prowler, and then realised that unless she betrayed Manuel she couldn't ask them.

However, with the burden of Jason's safety removed, there were other emotions to be dealt with. The prospect of facing him after what had happened between them the night before was no mean feat, and remembering her wanton behaviour she felt an overwhelming surge of humiliation. It was no use telling herself that he had been as much to blame. She had gone to his room, and had encouraged him to treat her like a tramp, and she could thank her stars that Miss Holland's intervention had saved her from herself.

How did one face a man after such an experience? she fretted. Her resourceful novel told of the cool-eyed captive spurning the advances of the passionate sheik, but not of his spurning her! Her breath caught in her throat. Was she so easy to ignore? Hadn't the love-making they had shared meant anything to him? And was Manuel really intended to be his replacement?

Smoothing velvet lounging pants over her hips, she jerked a pleated chiffon smock over her head and surveyed her appearance without appreciation. Was she too slim? she speculated critically. Were her breasts too small? And her hair, presently curling in moist tendrils about her temples, would it look better short? Manuel had not found her unattractive. On the contrary, she had recognised the expression in his eyes very well. Perhaps if she thought about him this evening, she could keep Jason's insensitivity at bay, and prove that her words spoken in the heat of the moment had meant nothing more to her than they had to him.

Downstairs, she found Miss Holland setting her delicious steak and kidney pie on the dining room table. Another cord to flay herself with, she thought bitterly, recalling her disastrous efforts of the previous evening. Jason and Ricardo had gone to change, Miss Holland told her, and Alexandra was more than eager to help with the vegetables, dreading that moment when Jason would appear.

She heard his voice first. He and Ricardo came into the dining room as she was laying serving spoons beside the tureens containing beans and carrots, peas and sweet potatoes.

'*Hola, señorita!*' exclaimed Ricardo at once, as she straightened to face them. 'You are looking flushed this evening, eh, *patrón?*'

It couldn't have been worse. Alexandra couldn't meet Jason's dark eyes, and it was left to him to say evenly: 'You're embarrassing her, Ricardo. I'm sure it's just the heat from the kitchen that has brought the colour to her cheeks.'

'Perhaps.' Ricardo was unrepentant. 'Or perhaps it is the

memory of the ride she took with my son this morning,' he teased. 'Manuel also was red-faced when I asked him about it.'

'Oh, yes . . .'

Jason sounded uninterested, and inclining his head thoughtfully, he turned away to take his seat at the head of the table. Only then did Alexandra chance a look at him.

In dark corded pants and a bronze-coloured silk shirt, he was disturbingly masculine, and she found it impossible to dissociate her thoughts from the disruptive memories the sight of him evoked. The thinness of his shirt barely disguised the shadow of the hair that she knew covered his chest in a fine cloud, and arrowed down his stomach to his navel; and the darkness of his wrists, projecting from his cuffs, drew her eyes to the long brown hands that had so urgently taught her the meaning of sensuality.

Miss Holland, coming into the room at that moment, provided a welcome distraction. She spoke to Jason, asking if he had any objection to her choice of a red burgundy to drink with the meal, and while they discussed the merits of various red and white wines, Alexandra slipped into her own seat beside Ricardo.

The food became the talking point, much to Alexandra's relief, although she waited apprehensively for Ricardo to make some joking comment about her disastrous efforts of the previous day. But whether or not Jason had warned him not to say anything, she didn't know. She only knew that for some reason the subject was taboo, and in that respect at least she was allowed to relax.

Once she encountered Jason's eyes upon her. It was towards the end of the meal, and he held her gaze for a matter of some five or ten seconds before averting his eyes. Yet for all that, she was left feeling unpleasantly disturbed by his appraisal, and she was glad when she could make the excuse of helping Miss Holland to clear the table. There had been contempt as well as anger in that stare, and she guessed he despised her now for what he considered her

promiscuity. As she loaded dishes into the sink, she
wondered if he expected her to behave that way with
Manuel. It was a bitter indictment, and she half wished she
were the kind of person able to indulge in those kind of
relationships. It would be a rough sort of revenge if she
could make Jason jealous that way, for while he might
abhor her behaviour, he could never deny the purely
physical needs she aroused in him.

The next morning Manuel appeared as she was helping
Miss Holland collect eggs from the hen-house. It was an
undemanding occupation, and she was thinking how hot it
was again and how nice it would be to plunge into the
cool waters of the river, when he sauntered into the yard.

'Buenos días, señoritas!' he greeted them gallantly,
sweeping off his hat in a theatrical gesture. 'It is a beautiful
morning, is it not?'

Miss Holland glanced reprovingly at Alexandra, and
then said shortly: 'Did you want something, señor?'

'Of course he did.' Alexandra stepped between them. 'You
know I asked Manuel to take me riding again today.'

Miss Holland snorted. 'To fall off again, I suppose,' she
exclaimed caustically, but Alexandra ignored her, demanding eagerly:

'What happened yesterday, Manuel? Did Jason find the
lion? I wanted to ask last night, but I couldn't.'

She had forgotten to explain to Manuel that Miss
Holland was in her confidence, but his eloquent expression
was indication enough. 'Oh, it's all right,' she added
apologetically, as he started making frantic gestures, 'Miss
Holland knows. But I haven't told anyone else. Honestly!'

Manuel was still very doubtful, but the desire to tell
what he knew overcame his scruples. 'They never even saw
her,' he said. 'She is a wily old beast, and the rain had
obscured her tracks. Maybe today . . .' He shrugged expressively.

In spite of the awful hollowness in the pit of her stomach
that his words had evoked, Alexandra had to behave

naturally. Besides, she was suddenly eager to get away from the house and its associations, and with a forced smile, she said: 'Let's go, shall we? I'll get my hat.'

'Alexandra!' Miss Holland's voice arrested her, and she glanced back reluctantly. 'Alexandra, where do you think you're going?'

'Riding. Where else?' Alexandra was offhand, but the older woman was not reassured.

'You wouldn't attempt to go looking for that—creature yourself, would you, Alexandra?' she exclaimed, unable to hide the note of anxiety in her voice, but this time it was Manuel who answered for her.

'We have more sense than that, *señora*,' he asserted quietly. 'Besides, if the *patrón* cannot find the old one, we assuredly will not.'

'We won't be long,' Alexandra promised. 'I'll be back to help you with lunch.' Then, her conscience pricking her, she added: 'Why don't you come with us?'

Miss Holland's homely features broke into a wry smile at this. 'Wouldn't you be disappointed if I said yes?' she countered teasingly. But she shook her head as Alexandra started to protest. 'No, my dear, not this morning. I'm a little tired. I think I'll get my book and sit here for a while, in the sun.'

Because it was so hot, Alexandra unfastened the neck of her shirt and rolled the sleeves above her elbows as the horses followed the track along the riverbank. Her thin jeans were clinging to her slender legs, but without them her skin would have suffered, and the brim of her hat was pulled low to protect her face. With the bees humming in the long grass, and the birds swooping and diving over the water, a reluctant feeling of well-being gripped her, and she determinedly put all thoughts of death and disaster out of her mind.

But Manuel, riding ahead of her, saw her thoughtful expression and misread it: 'You do not have to worry about the *patrón*,' he declared, and she looked at him in surprise.

'I know that is why you are so interested in the capture of the prowler,' he continued, as she made an offhand gesture. 'But Señor Tarrant has been in much tighter corners, believe me.'

'What do you mean?'

Alexandra spurred her mount until she was riding along beside him and Manuel explained: 'Did you not know he was once a soldier?' And as she shook her head, he went on: 'He was a—how do you say it?—a mercenary, yes? A soldier who fights for any country who can pay him.'

'I know what a mercenary is,' exclaimed Alexandra shortly. 'I didn't know that. When was this?'

'Oh, some years ago, I think.'

'Before he met my father?'

'Excuse me, I do not know of your father,' said Manuel doubtfully. 'But this was some—fifteen years ago, I think.'

'But he must only have been twenty or twenty-one at that time!' she protested.

'So? A man is a man. Whether he is twenty-one or fifty-one, he can still fight.'

Alexandra urged the chestnut ahead, digesting this without enjoyment. Her father had had no love of mercenaries, seeing them as heartless fortune-hunters, merciless killers, without even the saving grace of patriotism to excuse their bloodlust. Of course, her father had been an idealist, and any kind of violence was anathema to him. But nevertheless she felt there was some truth in what he said.

'So ...' Manuel came alongside her again. 'Does that relieve your mind?'

'Not really.' Alexandra moved her shoulders doubtfully, but not wanting to discuss her feelings with him, she changed the subject. 'Tell me, when will you decide whether or not you're going to take that job in Brazil?'

They rode every day that week, sometimes with Miss Holland, sometimes not, and Alexandra began to look forward to their outings. Manuel was a much more entertaining companion than his father had been, but perhaps that was because he was younger—and he flattered her. She knew he did, and while she accepted that his compliments were outrageous, it was good to feel that at least *he* found her attractive. Her relationship with Jason remained as ambiguous as ever. Because of his apparent indifference to her association with Manuel, he never referred to it, and those infrequent occasions when weakness made her try to heal the gulf between them brought a curt response. Yet, in spite of his attitude towards her, and the distasteful knowledge that he had made the money to buy San Gabriel out of other men's suffering, she was still as infatuated with him as ever. It was useless trying to pretend otherwise. Manuel was only a stopgap, someone to divert her thoughts from the blacker moods that came to claim her, but she had no desire for him to make love to her. They were good friends, and she was grateful for his friendship, but only Jason could 'set her aflame', a phrase she no longer had any difficulty in understanding. She dreaded Estelita's reappearance with all the agony jealousy could evoke, but so far there had been no word as to when she would return.

The mountain lion was still eluding capture, which curtailed the scope of their expeditions, and in spite of what Manuel had told her, Alexandra still fretted about Jason's safety. A diet of fictional adventures had alerted her to the dangers of an unexpected encounter, and she was always relieved when she heard him come home in the evening.

One morning, Manuel didn't arrive at his usual time. Alexandra, hot from helping Miss Holland clear out the *salón*, had been down to the river to dip her hands in the cooling water, and Chan's appearance on her return warned her that something was wrong.

'Manuel will not be coming today, *señorita*,' he told her apologetically. 'His father—he has need of him. They are fencing the western boundary, and he asks that you will excuse him.'

Alexandra let her shoulders sag. 'I see.'

'I am sorry, *señorita*.' And he obviously was, his olive-skinned face mirroring his regret. 'But you understand, his work must come first.'

'Of course.' Alexandra tried not to let the cook see how disappointed she really was. 'I'll see him tomorrow.'

At this, Chan looked discomfited, however. 'Maybe not,' he volunteered awkwardly. 'The *patrón*—he said it might take—several days.'

'The *patrón* did?' Alexandra's lips tightened. She might have known Jason had had some hand in this. What was wrong? Did he think she and Manuel were getting too close? Did he think it was time to call a halt to their relationship? Was he afraid she might corrupt one of his *innocent gauchos*?

She was so hurt and angry, she had to turn her face away from Chan so that he should not see the tears of frustration in her eyes. Fencing the western boundary! she thought bitterly. As if he hadn't enough men to handle that sort of work!

Watching Chan hurrying back to the bunkhouse, Alexandra felt a surge of indignation. So her outings were over for the time being, were they? When would they be started again? she wondered. When Jason considered that a suitable time had elapsed? Or when they killed the mountain lion and Ricardo could be recruited again?

It was so unfair, she thought moodily, scuffing her toe against a pebble. She and Manuel hadn't done anything wrong. They hadn't ridden into the mountains, or behaved irresponsibly. At least, Manuel hadn't, she conceded, remembering that first occasion when she had tumbled off the horse's back. Still, even Miss Holland had been favourably impressed by Manuel's politeness, and his courtesy to her as the older woman, and there was no reason why Jason should have taken it into his head to spoil their friendship.

Glancing back towards the house, Alexandra felt unsettled and restless. The idea of spending the morning sunning herself on the verandah had no appeal, and she looked longingly towards the stables. Jave had already saddled the mare in readiness for her departure, and now she would have to go and tell him she was not riding after all. Or would she?

Pushing her hands into the pockets of her jeans, she pulled a mutinous face. Why should she miss the outing just because Manuel wasn't here to accompany her? She knew the trails they followed as well as he did, and so long as she didn't stray off the beaten track . . .

She took a couple of steps towards the house to tell Miss Holland she was leaving, and then hesitated. She guessed without a shadow of a doubt, that the older woman would forbid her to go out alone, and unless she disobeyed her, all ideas of independence would be shattered. And why should she tell her, after all? She was behaving like the child she was constantly accused of being. Miss Holland didn't expect her back until eleven. There was no reason why she should even discover that Manuel had not gone with her.

Only Jave put up some opposition to her intention of riding off alone. '*A donde va usted?*' he exclaimed anxiously, looking round for the young man who usually accompanied her. '*Donde está Manuel?*'

'It's all right, Jave,' exclaimed Alexandra, speaking in his language with careful precision. 'I—er—I'm meeting him by the river.'

'*Qué?*' Jave was not entirely convinced, but when he let go of the bridle, Alexandra didn't wait to enter into any argument. With a wave of her hand she cantered out of the yard, leaving the old man to stare after her with evident misgivings.

The river had subsided considerably from the flood there had been after the storm. Now it was possible to cross at a shallower point Manuel had shown her, her feet splashing in the cool water as the mare waded almost shoulder-deep. On the far bank, there were clumps of poppies and dog daisies, and some of the sweet-smelling verbena that Miss Holland put to good use in the house. The grass was deeper

here, and the few cattle that grazed nearby paid little attention to her. Urging the chestnut up the gentle incline towards the few stunted bushes that bordered the trail worn
by generations of hooves, Alexandra decided she quite
liked the feeling that being alone gave her. She even per-
mitted a few strains of a favourite tune to pass her lips,
and a gurgle of excitement welled up inside her.

The trail wound between outcrops of granite and the
skeletal ribs of trees that struggled to survive in the rocky
subsoil. Far away to her right, the ridges of the higher
plateau beckoned, but she had more sense than to give in
to any adventurous impulses. The last thing she wanted
was for Jason to discover what she had been doing. It would
give her such a feeling of superiority, knowing she had out-
witted him at last.

Then her shoulders sagged. That wasn't strictly true. She
didn't really want to outwit him at all. Yet she knew she
was not likely to claim his attention any other way. Only
by defeating him at his own game was she likely to sustain
any feeling of self-respect.

When she estimated she had come far enough, she
climbed down from the mare's back, and tethering her to
some bushes, she seated herself on a smooth stone from
where she was able to view the whole length of the
valley spread out below her. It was incredibly beautiful,
and incredibly peaceful, and Alexandra felt a pang when
she considered that in a few short months this would no
longer be her home. Since Estelita's departure, she had
deliberately avoided thoughts of that kind, but it was impossible not to believe that the Spanish woman had been
right. And if Jason ever learned that she had been deceiving
him all along . . .

Determinedly, she turned her thoughts to less disruptive
matters. The previous evening Jason and Ricardo had been
talking about the yearly round-up of the mares and their
foals, and she had listened intently, wishing she might join
them on the trail. But there would be no question of that,

she knew. Jason would never trust her—*or himself*, she conceded dourly, realising that the intimacies of such a trip were such as he would want to avoid at all costs.

Depressed, she turned her head, and as she did so, she caught her breath. Standing on the track behind her, not ten yards away, was the black stallion. Her absorption in her thoughts had been such that she had not heard the drumming of his hooves, but now he had halted, nervously alert, aware of an intruder in his domain.

'Oh, you beauty!' breathed Alexandra huskily, rising slowly to her feet, and as she did so, the horse shifted sideways, its ears flattening against its head. 'Steady!' she whispered, half to herself as her fingers left the supporting warmth of the rock. 'I won't hurt you.'

The chestnut had lifted her head, and the stallion snorted, an arrogant sound, that echoed around the rocky slopes. Alexandra guessed it was the mare's scent he had followed, and she smiled as she considered what his thoughts must be at that moment. The mare made a protesting sound then, but as if sensing that here was one conquest he was not about to make, he turned, and with a whinny of annoyance, disappeared as abruptly as on those other occasions when she had seen him.

Hardly aware that she had been holding her breath, Alexandra allowed it to escape in a disappointed sigh. Just for a moment he had seemed to be responding to her tentative overtures, but then, with characteristic capriciousness, he had shown her exactly what he thought of her puny efforts.

Flopping back on to her rock, she plucked irritably at a blade of grass, catching it between her teeth, and chewing hard. Ricardo had said the horse was proud, and he was right. What were his exact words? *As proud as Lucifer!* She grimaced. Who could say for certain that Lucifer was proud? There wasn't much pride in being thrown out of heaven, was there? A fallen angel! She half smiled, as her irritation dispersed. That was what she would call him:

Fallen Angel. It was a title that fitted someone else she could mention . . .

The clatter of the mare's hooves on the stony track broke into her reverie. Jumping up in dismay, she saw that somehow the animal had broken loose from the bushes, and was presently making off along the track that the stallion had taken.

'Hey! You!' she yelled angrily, but the mare was far too intent on following the stallion's scent to pay any serious attention to her. 'Come back!' she commanded, but there was a futility to the words she uttered, and all of a sudden the idea of being alone had lost its charm.

It was miles back to the *hacienda*, and the thought of walking all that way filled her with alarm. Her shoes were strong and serviceable, but they were not boots, and Manuel had warned her often enough of the snakes that could still be found in the valley. Besides, the idea of crossing the river and getting soaked to the skin did not appeal to her, particularly as she could imagine Miss Holland's reactions if she came back dripping with water.

Even so, the idea of going after the mare was also a doubtful one. She had not forgotten the reason why Jason had forbidden them to ride into the canyons, and she would be courting disaster if she went on foot.

The sun, which until a few minutes ago had been deliciously warm on her shoulders, was suddenly uncomfortably hot, and not quite sure what she ought to do, she walked tentatively up to the point where she had seen the stallion. The clouds of dust still hanging in the air indicated clearly which way the mare had gone, and with a feeling of apprehension, Alexandra started after her. There was always the possibility that she might be waiting just around the bend in the trail, and remembering the lushness of some of the gullies, Alexandra quickened her step.

There was a grassy canyon, just beyond the ridge, and Alexandra thought she would never cease to marvel at the wonders of nature. Within this wall of rock and sandy topsoil was a green oasis, where a tumbling waterfall pointed the way to a sun-dappled pool. *A pool* . . .

Alexandra's tongue appeared momentarily to moisten her upper lip. How she longed to dip her face into its dark depths, and relieve the dryness of her throat with its pristine coolness. In her delight at finding the pool, she almost forgot her anxiety over losing the mare, but even though she looked all round there was no sign of her.

Time ceased to be of importance. She was going to be late anyway, so why worry over the few extra minutes it would take to scramble down the side of the ravine? If the mare was thwarted in her search for a mate, she might come back, and besides she was so thirsty . . .

The sides of the ravine were steeper than she had thought, and without the mare's sure-footed steps to guide her she slipped and slid most of the way on the seat of her pants. But at last she was standing beside the pool, stretching her hands into the falls, and it was only as she saw the scarlet stains colouring the water that she realised her palms were torn and bleeding. Pulling them back, she stared at them in dismay. They were a mass of cuts and abrasions, and they stung unbearably when the numbing influence of the water was withdrawn.

Turning her head, she gazed up the slope that she had just descended. With the first real twinges of panic, she wondered however she was going to climb back again. The sight of her hands had knocked her sick, and to imagine groping and grasping for holds on that scratchy face would be a daunting prospect at any time.

Ordering herself to remain calm, she made a careful survey of her position. She was standing just below the head of the ravine, where the pool formed a natural basin to catch the falls. Beyond, the waters spilled into a pebbly gully and ran away down the ravine, no doubt reaching the river in due course. *The river* . . .

Her heart quickened its beat. Of course, that was the answer. Sooner or later, the stream must reach the river,

and water did not flow uphill. The distances involved no
longer mattered. Just so long as she didn't have to use her
hands to save herself.

If only she had brought some food with her, she thought
unhappily. A bar of chocolate, or some fruit. Anything to
ease the nauseous emptiness inside her, which was made
more acute by her anxiety over the amount of blood she
was losing. One of the cuts was quite deep, and although
she bound it with her handkerchief, it still persisted in
seeping through.

It was a little after noon when she reached the end of
the ravine. The sun shimmering overhead had made mirages
of the solid wall of rock that confronted her, and the pass
she had expected to find was merely a dark chasm into
which the bubbling waters of the stream disappeared.

She stared aghast at that narrow cleft, slippery with
moss and overhung with creepers, realising that even if she
could squeeze herself inside, she would be blind to the
dangers within. She had no way of knowing what passage
the stream would take through the rock. No surety of being
able to make her way back again should the cleft become
too narrow for her. This was a box canyon, a perfect spot
for an ambush, and exactly the kind of place Jason had
warned them to avoid.

She was tempted then to sit down and weep. It had taken
over an hour to get this far and now to find it had all been
wasted effort was almost too much. She looked down at her
hands. They were trembling, but that was hardly surprising
considering her whole body was quivering with exhaustion.
Her handkerchief was soaked with blood, and on impulse
she bent down and rinsed it in the sparkling water, wincing
as she squeezed it out. At least, the cut looked clean, she
thought ruefully, realising the amount of blood she had
lost had disinfected the flesh, but it was still oozing, and
she wished she had something dry to wind around it.

Hunched beside the stream, she felt the unfamiliar pangs
of self-pity engulfing her. What if she couldn't make it

back to the trail? she fretted. How would anyone know
where to look for her? She scarcely noticed her acceptance
of the fact that someone would have to come looking for
her, and even the thought that it might be Jason no longer
had any fears for her. But this area was honeycombed with
canyons, Ricardo had told her that, and if they couldn't find
the mountain lion, why should they have any more success
with her?

A cold chill descended on her at this realisation. For
the past hour or so, she had been so intent on discovering
the way out of the ravine, she had almost forgotten why
Jason had forbidden them to ride in the mountains. Now
she glanced round apprehensively, half afraid she had in-
advertently found the jaguar's lair.

But she was alone. Behind her the slopes of the ravine
mocked the descent she had just made, its rugged contours
shifting and shimmering in the noonday heat. She couldn't
even see the waterfall from here, and her legs ached at the
prospect of the walk ahead of her. It was no use delaying
any longer, she realised. She was getting weaker all the
time she was without food and although her hands had
stopped bleeding, somehow she had to get out of this
canyon before the sun set.

Stumbling and sometimes falling, she began the gentle
ascent to the head of the ravine, stopping every now and
then to rinse her handkerchief in the stream. She made slow
progress, and all that kept her going was the knowledge
that Miss Holland would be desperately worried about her.
Jason might not yet know of her disappearance, and she
guessed Miss Holland might mount a search party without
telling him. She had not betrayed her before when she fell
from her horse, and she knew as well as anyone that Alexandra would want to avoid his censure. She made a silent
promise that if she came out of this alive, she would never
disobey Miss Holland again.

Once, as she knelt beside the stream, she saw flecks of
blood staining the grass. It was upsetting to think that she

had made those stains on her way down the ravine, wasting all that energy in a futile quest. It was strange, too, that in spite of the blood she had lost, her pulse was still pounding through her temples, throbbing in her ears . . .

A sudden scattering of stones behind her brought her abruptly to her feet. One pebble bounced across the turf to land almost at her feet, and with a gasp of horror, she closed her eyes. In those petrifying seconds, she was convinced the mountain lion had found her, and although she opened her mouth to scream, no cry emerged.

'Alexandra!'

Even the sound of her own name was an unreal intrusion into her terror, and not until it was repeated, with an added imprecation to God to be given strength, did she open her eyes to see Jason striding across the grass towards her.

She thought at first she was hallucinating, but somehow the drawn pallor of his features convinced her that this was Jason as she had never seen him before. He was hatless, his hair rough and uncombed, his shirt open down his chest to the low belt of his Levis. He was advancing down the slope towards her, and looking beyond him, she saw his horse and that of Ricardo waiting at the head of the ravine with the burly foreman. That was what she had heard, she realised, the pounding she had thought was in her head . . .

'Jason!'

Now in no doubt as to his reality, she extended her hands towards him, stumbling forward eagerly, and as he swept her into his arms, she heard his agonised: 'God, I could kill you!'

CHAPTER TEN

With her tearful face pressed to the moist skin of his chest, she could think of nothing but the heaven of being in his arms again. It was so long since he had held her, so many days and nights when she had thought he hated her, but now she was where she wanted to be, where she belonged. It didn't matter that the urgent way he was holding her was more in anger than any other emotion. He had been concerned about her, his trembling flesh told her that, and the sweating heat of his body spoke of the anguish he had suffered. With his hand at her nape, his fingers moving almost involuntarily among the damp curls, he was making a supreme effort to control himself, but the fierce throbbing of his heart would not subside so obediently.

Alexandra, for her part, clung to his strength with an urgency born of the torments she had experienced, uncaring of the pain to her torn and bleeding hands. Her whole body surrendered to the closeness of his embrace, and she had no thought for anyone but herself and Jason. She loved him, she *needed* him, and she didn't care if he knew it.

As if sensing her feelings, Jason would have pulled back then, but as he drew away from her, saying harshly: 'How much of this do you think I can take?' he saw the blood that stained his chest and smeared the clinging fabric of her shirt. His features contorting, he grasped her wrists, turning up the palms for him to see, and then caught his breath on a tortured groan.

'Oh, God!' he muttered, in a strange voice. 'So that's where it came from!' He bent his head to press his lips to her disfigured palms, his tongue gentle against the mutilated flesh. 'We—that is, Ricardo and I—found some blood on the rocks, up there.' He glanced impatiently up the

ravine. 'We thought—God! we didn't know what to think.'
He shook his head in painful remembrance. 'Alexandra,
Alexandra, what am I going to do with you?'

Her eyes clung to the beloved contours of his face.
'Wh-what do you want to do with me?' she whispered, and
his eyes closed over the torment that was mirrored there.

'Don't ask,' he muttered huskily, but when he opened his
eyes again, the uncertainty in her face tore away his last
vestiges of control. 'Oh, Alexandra ...' The words were
wrung from him, and this time when he jerked her close,
his mouth sought hers.

There was no thought of restraint. The agonies they had
both gone through had sharpened their senses, and they
kissed with a desperate passion. Repressions and inhibi-
tions were swept away by the urgency of a hunger long
denied, and the swelling hardness of Jason's body left her
in no doubt as to the effect she was having on him.

'When you didn't come back——' he got out thickly, his
hand sliding into the neckline of her shirt to probe the
rounded fullness of her breast. 'Have you any idea how I
felt?'

'I'm sorry, I'm sorry,' she breathed, his caresses almost
stopping the breath in her throat. 'I didn't want to worry
anyone, but the mare ran away, and I didn't know what to
do ...'

'You didn't know what to do!' he said dementedly,
cradling her hands against him. 'God, I nearly went out of
my mind!'

Alexandra looked up at him eagerly, lips parting in unconscious appeal. 'I—I thought you'd be so angry——'

'Angry!' He made a sound of frustration. 'Angry doesn't
describe my feelings at that moment. I just wished I had
you in my hands——'

'Like this?'

'No, not like this,' he groaned, his half-closed lids
shadowing the desire that burned in his eyes. 'I wanted to

shake you—or strangle you! Anything to prevent you from
—destroying me!'

She gulped. 'What do you mean?'

'Oh, Alexandra!' Shielding her with his body, he turned
to glance up to where Ricardo was watching, waiting . . .
'I've tried to ignore you, but I can't. I've tried to make you
hate me, but it doesn't seem to have worked very well,
does it?'

'I love you, Jason.'

'You think you do,' he retorted quellingly. With a determined effort, he pulled her shirt over her shoulders and
fastened the buttons. 'You're too young to know what you
want, Alexandra——'

'I'm almost eighteen.'

'Almost eighteen,' he echoed grimly. 'Alexandra, eighteen
is no age at all. You've done nothing yet, you've seen nothing of life. Living in a convent all those years! It wouldn't
be—fair for me to do what—what my instincts tell me to
do.'

'Which is?' she exclaimed breathlessly, but he shook his
head.

'That night,' he murmured, smoothing her hair back from
her damp forehead with slightly unsteady hands, 'that night
you came to my room, I would have made love to you, you
know that, don't you?' She nodded, and he went on: 'I
couldn't have stopped myself. I knew what I was doing
was wrong, but you were there, in my bed, and I wanted
you . . .'

'Then take me!' she pleaded urgently, but he shook his
head as he continued:

'Miss Holland breaking it up like that was a blessed
reprieve——'

'For you!'

'No, for you,' he contradicted her gently. 'If—if we had
slept together, I don't think I would have the strength to
let you go——'

'To let me go!' she echoed painfully, and his hands descended on her shoulders as she took an involuntary step back from him.

'Listen to me!' he urged tensely, and she was compelled to do so, albeit reluctantly. 'As I said before, you're too young! Me, I'm almost twenty years older. I've been around. I've seen something of the world—of life. I've even been married, although that was over long ago.'

That was a shock, and her lips trembled as she enquired tautly: 'Was that before or after you were a mercenary?' and his mouth turned down at the corners.

'Who told you that, I wonder?' he demanded. 'I can guess, of course. It was Manuel, wasn't it? Idealistic Manuel, with his youth, and his good looks, and his charm —and his irritatingly candid admiration for you!'

His words were harshly spoken and suddenly Alexandra thought she understood. 'You were jealous,' she said, only half believing it even then. 'Jason, you were jealous of Manuel!'

His grim features revealed a faint trace of self-derision. 'Yes,' he agreed, but there was no joy in the admission. 'Crazy, isn't it? A man of my age jealous of a girl scarcely out of the schoolroom!'

'Oh, Jason!' With a sob, she wound her arms around his neck again, laughing and crying together as relief bubbled up inside her. 'You don't have to be jealous of anyone, don't you know that? I don't care about Manuel. I love you! Only you.' She shook her head helplessly. 'Hold me,' she pleaded. 'Just hold me. I can't bear it when you turn me away.'

His arms came round her unwillingly at first, but the feel of her slim body straining against his was more than he could withstand. He could hear Ricardo shifting his feet impatiently on the ridge behind them, his spurs jingling audibly in the echoing reaches of the canyon; but the need to feel that warm mouth beneath his again overcame his scruples, and he knew that without Ricardo's presence he would have lost his head completely. As it was, the urgent demands of his own body drove him to part from her, the ache in his loins too painful to sustain.

'What am I going to do?' he groaned, dragging himself away to stare down at her with smouldering eyes. 'I can't let you stay here, feeling as I do. It would only be a matter of time before I——' He broke off abruptly, raking restless fingers through his hair, but his meaning was clear. 'There is only one solution, and I guess I've known it all along. I've got to send you back to England.'

'No——'

'Yes.' His firm submission overrode her horrified denial. 'It's all I can do—for my own sanity!'

She stared at him in hurt incredulity, and he shook her with gentle insistence. 'Don't look like that. It's not the end of the world. I'm not abrogating my responsibilities—I just think it would be the best thing—for both of us. A breathing spell, if you like. It needn't last for ever.'

'What do you mean?' Alexandra sniffed. 'You know that once I'm eighteen, your responsibility for me is at an end.'

'You think so?' His eyes darkened with emotion. 'You really think that your having a birthday is going to make that much difference to our relationship?'

'I—well, you can't go on supporting me after—after I'm of age.'

'Why not?'

'Because—oh, because you can't.' Alexandra bent her head, realising suddenly how fragile their relationship was. 'You know I'll have to get a job——'

'A job!' He made an impatient sound. 'You really think that your being eighteen cuts the ties between us? Dear God, have I said that? Have I given that impression?' He cast a resigned look in the foreman's direction. 'We can't talk here any longer. I've already condemned myself in Ricardo's eyes by touching you at all, and——'

'Condemned yourself?' Alexandra lifted her head to see the wry self-mockery that twisted his features.

'Yes.' He sighed. 'Ricardo's a religious man, although you may not have guessed it from the way he behaves sometimes. But he considers I'm too old for you, too, and he thought he'd found the perfect solution . . .'

Alexandra's tongue appeared. 'Then it was *his* idea . . .'

'. . . to substitute Manuel, yes.' Jason gripped her wrists as she would have moved closer to him. 'It was a good idea. Unfortunately, I couldn't take it.' His eyes dropped possessively down the length of her body. 'Maybe he'd have more sympathy if he knew what you do to me.'

'Oh, Jason!'

'Stay away from me, Alexandra,' he groaned, raising her palms to his lips once more. 'Don't make me despise myself any more than I do already.'

With an arm around her waist, Jason helped her up the rough incline to where Ricardo was waiting. His boots were firm on the shifting scree, and he dragged them up with clumps of turf until they were standing on the sandy track at the top of the ravine. Looking back, Alexandra shivered, but then Ricardo claimed her attention.

'What happened?' he demanded, and there was disapproval in every line of his bulky body.

Jason sighed again, taking hold of his horse's bridle. 'The mare made off,' he answered, and Alexandra realised her explanation had been far too brief for the length of time Jason had spent with her.

'I—I saw the stallion,' she offered, glancing awkwardly at her guardian. 'I'd dismounted for a rest and I guess I didn't tether the mare very securely.'

'Hah!' Ricardo snorted. 'If Manuel had been with you——'

'But he wasn't,' said Jason, and there was a hard quality in his voice that brooked no argument. Then he turned to Alexandra and indicated his mount. 'Come on. We'd better get back before Miss Holland has hysterics.'

'You did not seem so concerned for her welfare some minutes ago,' observed Ricardo caustically, and when Jason ignored him, he went on: 'What were you doing in the ravine, *señorita*? When we found the blood, we thought we had found——'

He broke off abruptly at that point, but Alexandra, now astride Jason's horse, turned to look at him. 'What did you think you'd found, Ricardo? The wounded mountain lion? Oh, yes——' this as Jason sucked in his breath in angry disbelief, 'I know about the prowler.'

'Then in God's name why did you go into the ravine?' snapped Jason, suddenly angry, swinging himself up behind her so that his hard thighs dug into her back. 'Who told you? Manuel, again? He should learn to keep his mouth shut.'

Even Ricardo looked sheepish at this, and Alexandra hastened on: 'It wasn't truly his fault. It just—slipped out.'

'Really?' Jason did not sound convinced, but he dug in his knees to urge the horse forward and Alexandra gave herself up to the pleasures evoked by the movement of his body behind her. They rode ahead of Ricardo out of the ravine, and as they did so, she saw the trail the mare must have taken snaking away around its rim.

Resting her head back against Jason's shoulder, she murmured softly: 'You're not really angry with me, are you? I didn't mean to worry anyone. I just wanted to—to——'

'—thwart me,' he finished huskily, his hand sliding over her midriff to the swelling mound of her breast. 'I'm not a fool, Alexandra.'

Her breath caught in her throat at his caresses, but she had to go on. 'I thought you despised me. I thought you stopped Manuel riding with me because you thought he might be—corrupted by my company.'

'Oh, God!' He bent his head to inhale the fragrance of her hair, and she felt his lips against her nape. 'If you only knew how I felt when you and Ricardo discussed those trips in the evening . . .'

Alexandra relaxed against him. 'Then you're not going to

send me away?' she breathed, but immediately, he stiffened.

'Six months,' he said, and her stomach contracted. 'Six months is a reasonable period. It will give you time to get things into perspective.'

'It will give you time, you mean!' she blurted hotly, and his fingers bruised the soft skin of her breast.

'No,' he contradicted savagely. 'I know what I want. But I respect your father's memory too much to abuse the trust he placed in me.'

Alexandra's hands clenched painfully. Now she should tell him the truth. Now she should reveal exactly how little trust her father had placed in him. But she couldn't. She couldn't!

'Miss Holland shall go with you,' he was continuing relentlessly. 'It will be winter here soon, but it's spring in England. Go to England, Alexandra. Have the summer to think it over. Come back to me at the end of the year, if you still want to.'

'If I still want to . . .' she whispered tearfully. 'Oh, Jason, you can't do this!'

'I assure you, I can,' he affirmed, and there was an implacability about him that separated them even as they rode together.

As if sensing it was now acceptable for him to ride with them, Ricardo came alongside at that moment, saying crisply: 'What a welcome home Estelita has had, no? Still, it is as well she is there to comfort the old one.'

With Jason's hand shifting to grip the pommel, he did not feel the retching upheaval of Alexandra's stomach, and she strove desperately for control. Until then it had not occurred to her to wonder how Jason had discovered she was missing, but with Ricardo's words she had her answer. When he left that morning, it had not been to go out with the men as she had imagined. He must have driven to Valvedra to fetch Estelita.

As if annoyed with the foreman for blurting it out like that, Jason explained quietly: 'Estelita's mother is making good progress. She sent a message yesterday, via the doctor at Puerto Novo, that she was ready to come home.'

To come home! The words tore into Alexandra's already shattered defences, ripping her to shreds with their intimate intonation. Home! Estelita's home. But not hers. *Never hers!* He was sending her away, just as Estelita came back, and the implications were impossible to avoid. She was almost glad when she saw the *hacienda* ahead of them, and when Miss Holland ran to meet them she wrenched herself away from Jason and down from his horse's back, to throw herself into the older woman's arms.

There were reproaches, of course, and recriminations, but the injuries to her hands were such that not even Miss Holland could remain immune from their vulnerability. Instead, she whisked Alexandra upstairs with the minimum of preliminaries, leaving Jason and Ricardo to explain what had happened.

But in the bathroom, with the door locked securely behind them, she gave vent to her feelings.

'You could have died!' she exclaimed, fussing over the cuts and scratches on her palms. 'You knew how I would feel if I discovered where you had gone, but you didn't care.'

'I did care,' protested Alexandra tremulously. 'Only— only——'

'Only you had to show Mr Tarrant how independent you were!' finished Miss Holland tersely. 'Oh, Alexandra! You should have heard the language he used to me when he discovered you were missing!'

Despite her misery, Alexandra couldn't help the sudden sense of excitement at Miss Holland's words. 'Why?' she cried. 'What did he say? Was that after he brought Estelita back?'

'He didn't bring Señora Vargas back,' retorted Miss Holland, dabbing at her hands tenderly with a swab of cotton wool, but Alexandra hardly felt the pain.

'He didn't?' she probed. 'Then who——'

'Señor Goya,' replied the older woman, concentrating on

her task. 'Mr Tarrant came home to take you riding. When he discovered you had gone, he was frantic. That was when Señora Vargas walked in.'

'Jason was going to take me riding,' echoed Alexandra faintly, closing her eyes against the images that evoked. 'Oh, Miss Holland! If only I'd known. If only I'd known!'

'Yes, well——' Miss Holland pursed her lips as she pulled another swab of cotton wool from the roll. 'You should know by now that Mr Tarrant goes to a lot of trouble on your account. It can't be easy for him. I know that.'

Alexandra licked her lips before taking her courage into her hands, and murmuring: 'What would you say if I told you—I was in love with him?'

There was silence for a few moments as Miss Holland sought for a tube of antiseptic ointment. Then, unwinding a sterilised bandage, she said: 'I would say that I guessed something was going on.' Her grey eyes were shrewd. 'Have you slept with him?'

Alexandra was flabbergasted. She had never expected the older woman to be so forthright. 'I—no. No, I haven't,' she admitted. 'He—thinks I'm too young.'

'He could be right,' remarked Miss Holland dryly, and then as Alexandra started to protest, she added: 'So? What does he intend to do about it?'

Alexandra hunched her shoulders. 'He wants me to go back to England—for six months.'

'Six months?' Miss Holland raised her eyebrows. 'An excellent suggestion, I should think.'

'An excellent suggestion?' cried Alexandra painfully. 'It's a terrible suggestion. He doesn't think I'll come back, that's what it is. He thinks that once I get to London I'll forget all about him.'

'You might,' said Miss Holland practically, applying the ointment to the bandage before winding it about her palm. But as the girl stared at her with tears in her eyes, she added: 'Then again, you might not. I take it he feels the same way?'

Alexandra hung her head. 'I—don't know.'

'Oh, come on. You must.'

'No.' She sniffed. 'He—he wants me, I know that. I think he needs me. But—love . . .' She shrugged helplessly. 'He's never said he loved me.'

Miss Holland nodded. 'I see.' She smoothed the bandage with expert care. 'But you must remember, Alexandra, it's harder for a man like him to admit to such a thing. I mean, he's not a boy. I hope you realise that.'

Alexandra's lips quivered. 'You sound so—experienced. Yet you've never married.'

'No.' Miss Holland applied herself to her task for a few taut minutes. Then she looked up. 'What would you say if I told you that the reason I never married was because the man I loved already had a wife?'

Alexandra gasped. 'Is that true?'

'As a matter of fact, yes.' Miss Holland reached for a second bandage. 'Like Mr Tarrant, he was a lot older than I was, but I wouldn't have had it any other way.'

'Did he love you?'

Miss Holland's smile was rueful. 'He said he did. And I think perhaps it was true, in a way. But he loved his reputation more.'

'Lord Carleon?' exclaimed Alexandra disbelievingly, and the faint colour that ran up Miss Holland's face was enough. 'Oh, Miss Holland! I'm so sorry.'

'Don't be.' Her companion was philosophical. 'It was all over years ago. Charles is almost eighty now, much too old to entertain those kind of fancies.'

'And did you—did you——'

Alexandra found she couldn't voice the words, but Miss Holland answered anyway. 'Did we have an affair?' she asked, and smiled. 'I suppose really I shouldn't tell you, should I?' She paused, and then seeing the girl's anxious face, she relented. 'We had a relationship,' she conceded. 'I'm not saying it was anything like the relationship you are having with Mr Tarrant. I didn't go around in skin-tight trousers or a shirt that exposed every curve of my bosom, but I did allow him to kiss me, and once we even went swimming together.'

'Would you—would you have married him if you could?'

'If he'd asked me,' agreed Miss Holland, with a sigh.

. 'Jason was married. He told me. But that was over a long time ago, too.'

Miss Holland completed her task and surveyed her handiwork critically. 'There, that should do,' she said, and Alexandra looked down at her bandaged hands.

'I look like a mummy,' she protested, depression at the remembrance of Estelita waiting downstairs overtaking her again. Then: 'What should I do?'

'What can you do?' retorted Miss Holland crisply. 'Do as he says. Go to England. Spend the summer there. If you love him, you'll come back, and if he loves you, he'll be waiting for you.'

'But what if he's not?'

Miss Holland shrugged. 'Isn't it better to know?' she asked, and Alexandra had to concede that she was probably right.

Alexandra didn't want any lunch, and spent the afternoon lying on her bed. She felt sick and disorientated, and even the news that Jason had gone to fetch the doctor from Puerto Novo to see her could not arouse her from her apathy.

Miss Holland brought the doctor up in the late afternoon. He smiled when he saw his patient and said half impatiently: 'If you do not care for yourself, *señorita*, perhaps you should care for the people who care for you. Señor Tarrant is most anxious about you. Did you lose a lot of blood?'

Alexandra twisted restively on the bed. 'Not a lot, no,' she replied, resenting his reproving tones. 'There was really no need for you to come, *señor*. Miss Holland has dealt with my injuries quite satisfactorily.'

The smile he cast in Miss Holland's direction was the

tolerant one exchanged between adults when a child is being unnecessarily fractious. 'Fortunately, Miss Holland understands the dangers of wounds of this kind,' he remarked. 'Tetanus is still an extremely dangerous disease, señorita. You would do well to remember that.'

The injection that followed was not pleasant, and Alexandra was left feeling helplessly near to tears. What was Jason doing now? she wondered. Would she see him again today? Or was she doomed to suffer Estelita's supercilious contempt while he drove the doctor back to Puerto Novo?

She was loath to go down for supper, but a determination to show the housekeeper she was not completely helpless made her bath and change into black culottes and a loose-fitting smock of black lace. She had never worn the outfit before, always secretly considering it too old for her, but tonight she felt she needed some defence.

However, when she came down the stairs, she found Jason standing in the hall. He was staring out into the blackness beyond the door, hands folded behind his back, and with a fast-beating heart she went to slide her bandaged palm into his.

Immediately he swung round, staring down at her intently, encasing her hands within the cool strength of his. 'Well?' he said, and there was more than anxiety about her health in his query. 'How do you feel?'

'Sore,' she answered at once, looking down at their hands entwined together. 'How about you?'

He didn't answer that, but asked instead: 'Was Miss Holland very angry?'

'She was more concerned with what you had said to her,' replied Alexandra unsteadily. 'I—I—you didn't tell me that Estelita was coming back today.'

'I was going to tell you this morning,' he answered. 'Did Miss Holland not tell you that I came back to take you riding myself?'

'Yes.' She darted a look up at him. 'I'm sorry, Jason. Oh, I always seem to be saying that to you.'

'Don't you?' he agreed. Then: 'Your hands—they're going to be all right?'

'Of course. They're not seriously injured,' she exclaimed, half impatiently. 'Jason—about going to England?'

'Yes.'

He released her hands then, thrusting his into his pockets, exposing the bulging muscles of his thighs. For a moment she gave herself the pleasure of just looking at him, and then his darkening expression forced her to go on.

'If—if that's what you really want me to do,' she got out jerkily, 'I—I'll do it.'

'I see.' There was a pregnant silence, and then he added curtly: 'Do I have Miss Holland to thank for this?'

It was almost as if he was disappointed with her submission. Alexandra stared up at him bewilderedly, trying to read the dark nuances of his expression, and then a voice she knew she would never be able to forget said silkily:

'Ah, the *señorita* is feeling better, no? How good it is to see you recovered, Miss Durham. I should not have liked you to miss supper on my first night home.'

They ate one of Estelita's meals—a stew of meat and vegetables, flavoured in the way she liked it. No mention was made of the scouring and cleaning which had gone on in her absence, and with a pang Alexandra realised that in the space of a day things had returned to normal. Except that Pepe was not with them. He had remained behind in Valvedra, with his mother, and would not be returning.

After Miss Holland's cooking, Estelita's left much to be desired, and Alexandra pretended it was this which closed her throat and left her feeling sick and miserable. But the truth was that the thought of leaving Jason was like a cancer inside her, eating away her emotions and leaving her weak and vulnerable. How could she contemplate six whole months without seeing him, without speaking to him, without being near him? It was an agonising prospect, and one which drove her constantly to seek his face, to imprint every angle of his features on her subconscious mind, so that when she looked away she could still see him.

Jason looked at her, too. She was not unaware of that, and when their eyes met, her stomach twisted with a feeling, half pain, half ecstasy. Then Estelita spoke, and when he turned to look at her Alexandra could have scratched her eyes out. Would Estelita still be here if she came back at the end of the year? she wondered despairingly. And if she was, what then?

When supper was over, Ricardo asked if he could speak to his employer, and with some reluctance Jason went with the foreman, leaving Alexandra alone with Estelita. Miss Holland had already gone into the *salón* to set out the chess pieces for later, and Alexandra was pushing back her chair, preparatory to leaving the table, when Estelita pulled a letter out of her blouse and threw it across to her.

'Here,' she said. 'I collected Jason's mail before leaving Valvedra. I thought this one might be of some interest to you.'

'To me?' Alexandra turned the parchment envelope over in her fingers. 'Why should it—*oh!*'

She broke off abruptly as she recognised the small neat handwriting, but its precise quality was unmistakable, as was the plain convent envelope.

'I see you know where this letter comes from,' observed Estelita slyly. 'Perhaps you wonder why the convent at Sainte Sœur should be writing to your guardian, *no?*'

Alexandra frowned. 'How do you know where it's from?' she exclaimed. 'The letter's addressed to Jason, and it's sealed. You—you opened it!'

'You should be thankful that I did, *señorita,*' retorted Estelita coldly. 'For I know what is inside it, and I am sure Jason would be very interested to hear that your father wanted you to return to the convent when he died.'

Alexandra blanched. 'What do you mean?'

'I mean, *señorita*, that the good sisters at the convent know nothing of any plans to put you in Jason's care.'

Forcing herself to remain calm, Alexandra defended herself. 'Why should they?' she countered. 'They were not involved——'

'Oh, but they were, *señorita*.' Estelita's face had taken on the grotesque quality of a mask. 'You see, your father telephoned the good sisters only two days—*two days*—before he died, telling them of his wishes, advising them that his solicitors would be in touch with them.'

Alexandra was trembling now, but she dared not let Estelita see how shocked she was. 'I don't believe you,' she said jerkily. 'Why should I believe you?'

'Why should I lie?' retorted Estelita contemptuously. 'Open the letter for yourself. See what is written in it.'

Alexandra shook her head, turning the envelope over in her fingers. 'It's addressed to Jason.'

'Yes, it is,' Estelita nodded. 'And can you imagine what his reactions will be when he reads it? When he learns that *you* tricked him. Oh, yes, *señorita*, I have had time to work it all out. *You* wrote the letter to the solicitors which purported to have come from your father. *You* made Jason your guardian. Why, I wonder? You had never met him. Were you so desperate for a man, *señorita*?'

Alexandra's chair thudded on to the floor behind her as she sprang to her feet. 'Don't you dare say such a thing to me!' she declared tremulously. 'You wouldn't understand. You wouldn't understand in a million years!'

Estelita sneered, 'You think Jason will?'

Alexandra trembled. 'I don't know ...' She said the words almost inaudibly, as much to herself as anyone else.

'Then I will tell you, *he won't*!' declared Estelita coldly. 'No man likes to be made a fool of, particularly by a slip of a girl young enough to be his daughter!'

Alexandra put a hand to her head. It was swimming, and she wondered if the antibiotic the doctor had given her was responsible for her dizziness. Or perhaps it was because she had had nothing to eat all day. Whatever, she felt sick and confused, and Estelita was only voicing what she had feared all along.

'Why—why did you show me this letter?' Alexand.
asked now, supporting herself against the table. 'Why
haven't you given it to Jason?'

Estelita rose now. 'I had my reasons.' She placed the
palms of her hands squarely on the table. 'I want you to
leave here, señorita. And I do not care what methods I
have to use to achieve that objective.'

'I don't—understand——'

'I will explain.' Estelita was very much the mistress of
the situation at that moment. 'As I have said, Jason would
not like to think you had made a fool of him. Can you
imagine how he would feel if the men—the gauchos—
learned that you had tricked your way into his house? He
would be—how do you say?—a laughing stock, no? Do
you think he would like that?'

'No!'

'No. So I think to myself, there is no reason why he
should see the letter, why anyone should see the letter, but
our two selves. If you agree to leave without fuss, I will
destroy it, and you can explain the situation to the nuns
after you have returned to England.'

'You mean—you're blackmailing me?' Alexandra had to
get this straight. 'If—if I don't agree to leave, you'll make
this letter public?' She caught her breath on a sob. 'Aren't
you afraid of what Jason will say when he learns you've
been reading his mail?'

Estelita shrugged. 'So—he is angry! So what? He needs
me here. He is not likely to dismiss me because of a little
thing like that, is he?'

Alexandra pressed her lips together to hide their trembling. 'What—what if Jason won't let me go?'

Estelita's mouth thinned to an ugly red line. 'I saw the
blood on his clothes today, señorita. I know what you have
been trying to do while I have been away. But I also know
what you said to him in the hall before supper, and I do
not think he will stand in your way.'

Alexandra pressed a hand to her stomach. 'You think you

ve all the answers, don't you? But—but what will you do
I come back?'

'My—*husband* and I will always welcome guests into our
home,' retorted Estelita mockingly, and Alexandra gasped.
'Oh, yes, he will marry me, *señorita*,' she added. 'Even if I
have to become pregnant to force his hand.' Her lips curved
sensuously. 'He is so careless about these things, you
know. He relies on me entirely. You understand?'

Alexandra understood. She understood only too well,
and the knowledge almost robbed her of the strength to
leave the room. But somehow she had to get away—away
from Estelita, away from San Gabriel, and most important
of all, away from Jason . . .

CHAPTER ELEVEN

THE furnished house Miss Holland had leased was in a fashionably attractive square in Belgravia. Tall and narrow, its Georgian façade stretching skywards, it was more grand than anything Alexandra had expected, but her companion had told her that Jason had insisted on their being comfortable. Area steps to the side of the door led down to a basement flat occupied by the housekeeper and her husband, and Mrs Beesley, as the housekeeper was called, kept everywhere in spotless order. The house was really too big for two women living alone, but Miss Holland said that flats were soulless places, and she at least appreciated its luxury.

Alexandra showed little interest in her surroundings. She had shown little interest in anything since their departure from South America, and spent most of that first week with her face buried in a book. There was a comprehensive library at the house in Mountsey Square, and in those early days she spent most of her time there, despite Miss Holland's admonitions to get out into the watery spring sunlight.

Since that terrible scene with Estelita, she had had plenty of time to think, and her thoughts were not pleasant. Too often she was brought back to the conclusion that Jason's prime objective in persuading her to leave was because of the housekeeper. He had been attracted to her, it was true, and during Estelita's absence his natural appetites had not been appeased. That was why he had turned to her, why she had found it easier to arouse him. But once he knew Estelita was coming back, he had realised he could not satisfy two women without one of them becoming jealous. That was when he had decided that Alex-

must leave. All that talk about his not being able to
her feeling as he did, his protestations of wanting only
e best for her, and the need for her to get things into
perspective, had all been a blind, a clever ruse to persuade
her to do what he wanted. He had known that once he got
her out of the valley, she would not return uninvited, and
in the meantime, Estelita had her own plans for the master
of San Gabriel.

Things had moved quickly once Alexandra had agreed to
go. She was never quite sure who arranged that they should
leave at the end of that week, but Jason seemed curiously
indifferent to the whole situation. It was Estelita who re-
layed that a flight had been booked for them on the Friday
morning, and it was arranged that Ricardo should drive
them to Valvedra.

On Thursday evening, Jason asked Miss Holland if he
could have a few words with her in his study once supper
was over. Alexandra, who had half hoped he would include
her in the invitation, was left to face the unpalatable realisation that so far as Jason was concerned she was still a
child, and as such, not worthy of inclusion in their dis-
cussions. She guessed he was giving Miss Holland instructions for their journey, and that lady's later revelations that
they were to spend the first few days at an hotel while she
looked for a suitable house to lease confirmed this assump-
tion. Alexandra went to bed without seeing Jason again, and
the first painful seeds of distrust were sown.

Although she hardly slept that night, first light found her
down at the stables, saying goodbye to Jave. She bestowed
a tearful kiss on his gnarled cheek before bidding farewell
to Placida, the little mare who had so patiently borne her
first stumbling efforts. She couldn't say goodbye to the
chestnut mare. She had not returned, and she hoped with
all her heart she would not fall victim to the jaguar, who
still ran free somewhere in the mountains.

Her farewell to Jason was a stilted affair. He appeared
as she was having breakfast, and seemed irritated to find

her already at the table. Perhaps he had hoped
break down, she thought maliciously, cloaking he.
ability in a shell of indifference. Well, she wouldn
would not give him that satisfaction.

Instead, after Ricardo had loaded their cases into tr.
Range-Rover and Miss Holland had said her goodbyes,
Alexandra held out her hand for Jason to shake, and saw
the kindling anger in his eyes. It was as if they were
strangers, she thought, unfriendly strangers, wary of further
contact.

But short of causing a scene, there was little he could
do, she realised that. She realised, too, that he had probably
expected to kiss her goodbye. He had enjoyed kissing her—
he had made no secret of that fact. And she was glad of
the little victory her coldness afforded. But once aboard the
Boeing that lifted off the airport at Valvedra, she locked herself in the toilet and gave in to the weakness of tears.

To begin with, she had cried a lot, usually into the
secrecy of her own pillow, and her face grew pale and
drawn. But gradually her vulnerability gave way to a certain
hardness, a cynical contempt for her own immaturity, that
gave her the strength to go on. Jason had been an experience, she told herself coldly. Her *first* experience—and the
one and only time she would give her heart to anyone.

This decided, she gave herself up to a determined effort
to enjoy life again, but by the end of her first month at
Mountsey Square, she knew she was bored. Miss Holland's
outings to museums and theatres bored her, as too did the
prospect of spending the rest of her life searching for
artificial pleasures. She had never been used to needing
entertainment on the grand scale. At the convent, she had
had to amuse herself, and her thoughts had never been a
trouble to her as they were now. It was frightening to
realise that what she was really trying to do was fill her
days so that she would have no time to think, and that was
no life at all.

But she hated London, with its close, narrow streets and

. It gave her a feeling of claustrophobia, and ⸻d for the open spaces of the *pampa*, and the feel ⸻mare's strong muscles between her thighs. It took ⸺ome time to realise it, but gradually it came to her ⸺t what was really happening was that like the recurrence of some awful disease, she was having a second attack of homesickness for San Gabriel, and Jason. It was useless telling herself she hated him. The longer they were apart, the harder it became to put him out of her mind. And no matter how he had treated her, she would never forget him.

That was when she decided she would have to get a job. But what? A discussion with Miss Holland was not satisfactory, since that lady proffered the belief that Alexandra should give herself more time before rushing into anything so binding as a career. Wait until the end of the summer, she said, knowing nothing of that terrible scene Alexandra had shared with Estelita. What had happened to her determination to return to South America? Was she already regretting that decision, or had she some other plan in mind?

Alexandra put her off with vague excuses that she was not happy doing nothing, that she would prefer to be occupied, and hoped that sooner or later it would filter through to the older woman that all was not as straightforward as it had at first seemed. It was too soon to talk about her future, she averred, realising as she did so that Miss Holland would probably think she had changed her mind, and put it down to her extreme youth.

The six-months lease on the house had been paid by Jason, but Alexandra decided that as soon as she had regular employment, she would suggest to Miss Holland that they moved into a flat of her choosing. She realised that Jason was paying Miss Holland's salary, and she couldn't be absolutely sure what that lady would do once Alexandra broke free of her guardian, and for the present she had to accept his largesse. But she still had the nest-

egg provided by the sale of her father's house, a~
that would provide enough funds to furnish a smal~
ment when the need arose.

She said none of this to Miss Holland, however. T~
older woman was enjoying a well-earned rest, revisiting al~
her old haunts and meeting up with old friends. After her
strenuous stint at the *hacienda*, she deserved a break, and
there was no point in worrying her unnecessarily.

During those early weeks Alexandra had visited her
father's solicitors and cleared up the matter of her father's
letter. She crossed her fingers as she maintained that he
must have forgotten having written to Jason, and as she
was obviously fit and well cared for, the elderly solicitor
was more than willing to let the matter drop. He would
write to the convent, he promised, and she left his office
feeling an overwhelming sense of relief.

It wasn't easy finding a job, however, without either
references or qualifications. Office jobs all needed good
passes in English and an ability for typewriting which Alexandra did not possess, and the more menial type of post
paid such low wages. She realised if she wanted to earn a
salary suitable to maintain a reasonable standard of living,
she would have to go back to school and take examinations,
and while she was willing to do this, there were no courses
starting again until September.

In consequence, she eventually accepted a job as a
waitress in a coffee bar in Chelsea. It wasn't a very fashion-
able coffee bar, and it was owned by a rather sleazy-looking
Greek called Stefanos, but at least it meant she had somewhere to go through the long daylight hours.

Miss Holland was horrified. She had never dreamt Alexandra would go through with actually taking such a job,
and her disapproval was more than eloquent.

'How do you think I feel, knowing you're working in that
dreadful place?' she protested. 'What will Mr Tarrant think
when he finds out I'm living here in the lap of luxury, while
you're spending every day in that unhealthy atmosphere?'

don't care what Mr Tarrant thinks,' Alexandra
tautly, adding cream to the coffee Mrs Beesley had
after dinner that evening. 'As—as a matter of fact,
rather you didn't tell him.'

She knew Miss Holland was obliged to write a weekly
report to her employer, and she had often wondered what
she found to write about, but in this instance she would
rather her affairs remained private.

'I don't understand you,' exclaimed Miss Holland now,
shaking her head. 'Less than two months ago, you told me
you loved him, and now, here you are, taking a job you
know he wouldn't approve of, and asking me not to tell
him!'

Alexandra heaved a sigh. 'Yes, well—I've been meaning
to tell you about that,' she mumbled unwillingly. 'I—Jason
and I—we're washed up—finished. You know—it's all over.'

'All over?'

Miss Holland stared at her disbelievingly, and Alexandra
closed her eyes against the astonishment in her expression.
'Yes,' she insisted, pressing a hand to her churning stomach.
'I've wanted to tell you for some time, but—well, you know
how it is.'

'No, I don't know how it is,' retorted Miss Holland impatiently. 'Alexandra, are you telling me you've changed
your mind?'

'And if I was?'

'I wouldn't believe you.' Miss Holland's fists clenched.
'Good heavens, girl, you're eaten up with love for that
man, even I can see that! I just don't understand what
you're trying to do.'

Alexandra rested her elbows on the table and rested her
chin on her knuckles. 'You don't have to understand,' she
said unevenly. 'It's over, I tell you. He doesn't want me. He
never did. I was just a—a diversion while Estelita was
away.'

'You don't believe that!'

'I do. I do.' Alexandra sniffed, feeling the smarting sting

of tears behind her eyes. 'If you only understood . . .'

'Understood? What's to understand?'

'About—about Estelita . . .'

'What about her?'

'She—Jason's going to marry her.'

'I doubt that, very much.' Miss Holland looked disbeliev-ing. 'If he had been going to marry Estelita, he'd have done so before now.'

'Well, she wants to marry him.'

'Might I remind you, I wanted to marry Lord Carleon? Much good it did me.'

'But if—if you'd been pregnant . . .'

'Estelita's not pregnant!'

'No, but she might be.' Alexandra caught her lower lip between her teeth. 'If she—let it happen . . .'

'You're implying that Mr Tarrant would be responsible?'

'Yes.'

Miss Holland snorted. 'I never heard anything so fanciful! Do you honestly believe that a man like Mr Tarrant, with his experience of the world and its vagaries, wouldn't take damn good care something like that didn't happen unless he intended it to do so?'

Alexandra stared at her, her lips trembling. 'You accept then that they do sleep together?'

'I don't accept any such thing. I'm not saying that they might not have, in the past. She's obviously willing, and Mr Tarrant is very much a man, after all.'

'Oh, Miss Holland . . .' Tears oozed down Alexandra's cheeks. 'If only you were right!'

'Well, at least give me the benefit of the doubt.' Miss Holland leant across to pat her arm. 'My dear, surely you're not going to let a woman like Estelita keep you from finding out the truth for yourself?'

'How?'

'Go back at the end of the summer. See—Jason.' It was the first time Miss Holland had used his given name. 'Do that, if you do nothing else.'

Alexandra rubbed her palms across her cheeks, noticing as she did so how the scars were fading. They were pale, of course, and still very painful if she used them unwarily, but no longer raw and vulnerable. If only the same could be said for her!

'You don't know everything,' she admitted at last, when Miss Holland continued to look at her with expectancy. 'I lied to Jason. All the time I was at San Gabriel, I was living a lie.'

Miss Holland frowned. 'Go on.'

Alexandra hunched her shoulders. 'Well ...' she began reluctantly, 'my father didn't write that letter asking Jason to be my guardian, I did.'

'You?'

'Yes.' Painfully, Alexandra explained the situation, making no excuses for her behaviour. 'I didn't want to go back to Sainte Sœur. I just wanted to be free,' she finished lamely, and Miss Holland felt a surge of sympathy for this girl who had known no other life but that of the convent.

'Why didn't you tell Jason?' she asked now, squeezing Alexandra's arm. 'I'm sure he'd have understood. I'm sure he *will* understand.'

'No.' Alexandra shook her head. 'There was a letter, you see. Estelita brought it that day she came back from Valvedra. It was from the convent. They—they must have contacted Daddy's solicitors, and learned that he was dead and that I was living in Santa Vittoria. At any rate, they had written to Jason, telling him that my father had telephoned *them*, asking them to look after me when—when he died.'

'Who told you this?'

'Can't you guess? Estelita. She had opened the letter, you see. She showed it to me, but not to Jason.'

'Where is the letter now?'

'Estelita destroyed it, I suppose. I don't know. I never saw it again after that night she came back to San Gabriel.'

'I see.' Miss Holland was thoughtful.

'Do you?' asked Alexandra now, shifting on her
'Can't you see how Jason would react if he learned the t
He—he never wanted to take me to San Gabriel, you kn
that. If he found out I'd deliberately deceived him . . .'

'Nevertheless, I think you should tell him,' declared
Miss Holland at last. 'If, as it appears, you do not intend
to return to San Gabriel, what have you to lose?'

'No.' Alexandra shook her head. 'No, I couldn't do that.'

'Why?'

'Estelita threatened to make the letter public knowledge
if I didn't leave the *hacienda*. She said Jason would hate
being made to look a fool.'

'What a nasty piece of work she is!' exclaimed Miss
Holland impatiently. 'I can't imagine why Jason ever made
her his housekeeper.'

'She was a widow, and she needed the work,' replied
Alexandra practically. 'Besides, not everyone would want to
live so far from the city.'

Miss Holland nodded. 'That's true, of course. And I suppose she does care for him in her own way. Even so, I
think he deserves to know the truth. Perhaps I should——'

'No. Oh, no.' Alexandra shook her head again. 'Don't do
anything. This is between me—and Jason. Whatever happens, I have to handle this myself.'

It was approximately two weeks later that Alexandra had
an unexpected visitor to the coffee bar. She was clearing
tables when a voice behind her said: '*Buenos días, señorita.
Cómo está usted?*'

She swung round eagerly, half believing it might be
Jason, to gaze in amazement at Manuel Goya. 'Manuel!'
she exclaimed bewilderedly. 'Heavens, what are you doing
here?' Her eyes darkened. 'Do you have bad news? Is
anything wrong? Is Jason well?'

'No, no, and yes,' he responded, his eyes twinkling with
wry amusement. 'That answers your questions, *si*? As to
why I am here, I came to see you, of course.'

out . . .' Alexandra glanced round nervously. 'How
u find me? What are you doing in London?'

anuel smiled. 'We cannot talk here, in the middle of a
ifee house. Can you have lunch with me?'

Alexandra hesitated. 'Lunchtime is our busiest time,' she
confessed. 'I could have dinner with you this evening.'

'Unfortunately, that is not possible,' said Manuel sadly.
'I am passing through London on my way to Rome. I have
to leave on this evening's flight.' He sighed. 'I did not
realise you had a job. Jason did not tell me.'

'Jason doesn't know,' said Alexandra unhappily. 'Oh,
Manuel! If only I'd known you were coming!'

'Si.' He looked disappointed, too. Then his expression
lightened a little. 'I know,' he said. 'I will have lunch here,
at the coffee bar, *no*? Then, in between times, we can talk.'

It wasn't very satisfactory, but it was the best they
could do. Alexandra was kept busy from twelve o'clock on-
wards, but in between serving hamburgers and toasted tea-
cakes, she managed to snatch a few words here and there.

It appeared that Manuel had taken his father's advice at
last, and was working for the Fredrikson organisation. Because the firm had offices in Rome, Manuel was being sent
there for three months to learn European methods of
engineering, and it had been his father's suggestion that he
stop off in London to see Alexandra. Knowing Ricardo's
pride in his son, Alexandra guessed the older man had
wanted her to see how successful Manuel had become, and
maybe he hoped that their friendship would develop now
that there were fewer miles between them. It was sad, she
thought, that Manuel had not been the one to capture her
heart. He would have been so much easier to love.

Once in London, Manuel had gone straight to their
address in Mountsey Square, and from Miss Holland he had
learned where she was working. Like her, he was distressed
that Alexandra should not have asked Jason's advice before starting on such a career, but he gave an unwilling
promise not to interfere.

Talking about Jason was less easy, Alexandra found. It was difficult to ask the questions she wanted to ask without giving away her feelings, but it seemed that the situation at San Gabriel was much as usual. At least he was not married, she thought with relief, although she acknowledged bitterly that such things took time. Nevertheless, so long as he remained unmarried, she could entertain thoughts of going back there, even if the chances of her doing so were slim indeed. Jason had never written to her. So far as she knew, he had never even sent a message to her. And he must know that she could never return without his invitation.

Manuel left to catch his plane, and Alexandra watched him go with a terrible sense of isolation. For a time, she had felt close to Jason again, and hearing Manuel talk about the *estancia* and its problems had brought it all into painful focus. But now he had gone, and she was left with the unpalatable knowledge of her own duplicity. If only she had told Jason right at the beginning! she thought despairingly. If only she had confessed to her ploy before the letter arrived, condemning any hope of his forgiveness.

June was a hot month in London, and working in the sweaty atmosphere of the coffee bar, Alexandra was sapped of all strength by the time she got home. She didn't even have the energy to go seeking a flat, and the realisation that in less than three months the rent on the house would fall due again filled her with anxiety. She could pay it, she supposed, using the money her father had left her, but it would take a sizeable slice out of the funds she had hoped to use to furnish her own apartment. Besides, there was Mrs Beesley's wages to consider, too. She was part of the deal, without the added burden of what they would eat. That was a detail Jason had not neglected in his arrangements with Miss Holland, and knowing the price of food, Alexandra dreaded the thought of how much money he had already spent on them.

many problems, she reflected wearily, in her lower its. And all of them seemingly insoluble. Perhaps she ould have stayed at the convent. Life there had been uneventful, it was true, but at least she had not had this burden of guilt to bear. Perhaps she ought to write and ask the nuns if they would take her back. Sanctuary sounded very sweet to someone robbed of all self-respect.

Because she started work at eight-thirty, Alexandra was always up first in the mornings. Mrs Beesley would prepare her coffee and toast, and then disappear downstairs to attend to her husband's breakfast. Mr Beesley worked as commissionaire to a block of offices, and Alexandra sometimes saw him when she was leaving, erect and military-smart in his uniform. He would raise a hand in greeting, and she would wish him 'Good morning', and then they would go on their way, she to walk to the coffee bar, and he to catch the tube to the Barbican.

One morning towards the end of June, Alexandra slept in, and it was gone eight-thirty when she came down the steps of the house. Seeing the man coming up the area steps, she thought Mr Beesley must have slept in, too, and she had opened her mouth to commiserate with him before she realised that the thick dark hair and sun-bronzed skin were not those of the housekeeper's husband. Besides, the expensive suede suit was not the sort of thing a man in his sixties would wear, and the broad shoulders and lean, muscular body moved with the lithe grace of a much younger man.

Although she needed no second look to recognise who it was, Alexandra could not drag her eyes away from him, and it was only as she felt the metal of the handrail digging into her still-tender palms that she realised she had paused in mid-flight.

Jason climbed the area steps and halted on the path below her, tall and disturbingly familiar. She realised she knew every detail of his face, from the lines that bracketed his mouth to the thickness of his lashes, and his nearness was almost her undoing. She wished he would speak, wished he would say something—anything—to expl. what he was doing there, and whether he was alone. H. seemed tired, she fretted anxiously, and perhaps he had lost a little weight, but he was still the only man who could send the blood thundering through her veins, and turn her bones to water.

'So you are up,' he commented at last, hardly the words she had expected him to use, and she nodded jerkily, saying:

'Actually, I'm late. I'm usually out of the house before this. Unfortunately, I slept in.'

She didn't add that the reason she had overslept was because she had cried herself to sleep the night before, but Jason's shrewd gaze lingered on the dark rings around her eyes, and the slight puffiness that betrayed her distress.

'Oh, yes . . .' Jason put his foot on the first step and came a little nearer. 'Your famous job at the coffee bar. I hadn't forgotten about that.'

Alexandra gasped. 'How did you know I had a job? Oh, I see . . .' Her mouth took on a mutinous curve. 'Miss Holland told you. She promised——'

'Miss Holland didn't tell me a thing,' contradicted Jason flatly, taking another step until there was only the space of one slab of concrete between them. 'Although I would have expected her to, knowing I trusted her.'

Alexandra stepped to one side. 'Well, if that's why you've come——'

'It's not,' he retorted, sidestepping himself to block her path. 'Shall we go inside?'

Alexandra drew a deep breath. 'I—I can't. I've just told you, I'm late. Mr Stefanos doesn't approve of unpunctuality. I'm sorry if you've chosen the wrong time to catch me——'

'I didn't choose the time,' he told her, deliberately taking the final step that brought his body into touching distance of hers, or would have done if she had not hung back. 'I came straight here from the airport.' He glanced at his

..'I arrived from Rio a little over an hour ago.'

...lexandra's mouth was dry. She didn't know why he had
.me, or how he had found out about her job. Unless it was
.rom Manuel. But he had promised not to interfere . . .

'Jason, please——'

'No. You please—me!' he declared harshly, and reached
for her handbag. 'I assume you do have keys in here, do
you?'

'Don't! I mean—you have no right . . .'

'Don't I?' His tone was grim. 'I think your landlord
would disagree with you there,' he retorted, and finding her
key, he inserted it in the lock.

'Oh, you—you——' Alexandra could think of no adjec-
tive suitable to her opinion of him in that moment, strip-
ping away as he was her last vestiges of self-respect, but
Jason wasn't even listening to her. Instead, he caught her
wrist in a vice-like grip when she would have escaped him,
and practically dragged her into the hall behind him.

'If you think because you pay the lease——' she began
tremulously, as the door slammed shut behind them, but
Jason pulled her after him, across the hall and into the
sunlit elegance of the drawing room. Only then did he release her, but he made sure she was in the centre of the
room, while he positioned himself behind the closed door.

'Now,' he said, folding his arms, 'before we discuss the
matter of your resignation, suppose you tell me how you
perpetrated this little fraud?' And from his pocket he
drew the small white envelope with Reverend Mother's
handwriting upon it.

Alexandra's legs were like jellies as she stared at that
small square of parchment. He had found out, then, she
thought dully. Even though she had left San Gabriel, even
though she had cut herself off from everything she held
most dear, Estelita had still found it necessary to betray
her.

'That—that's a letter from Sainte Sœur,' she murmured,
playing for time. 'I—I recognise the handwriting.'

'Do you?' He inclined his head. 'I believe you also
what the letter contains.'

'I—well, I know of it,' she faltered. Then, as if appealir
to him at this late date would do no good, she added: 'I—
I'm not ashamed of what I did. It—it was worth it, even if
—even if you do despise me now. I—I would do it again . . .'

'Would you?' He raised dark eyebrows.

'Yes. And—and Estelita promised me you would never
see that letter.'

'Let's leave Estelita for the time being, shall we?' Jason's
mouth tightened. 'I'd like to know how you managed to
get your father to write that letter.'

'Oh.' Alexandra was disconcerted. 'Well, I—I wrote all his
letters for him, you see. He—he didn't have a steady hand,
and he only signed them.'

'Ah,' Jason nodded. 'Now I begin to understand.'

'I—I wanted to tell you,' she said wretchedly, needing to
say something. 'But you already resented the responsibility . . .'

'Did I do that?'

'You know you did.' She sighed. 'If only I'd been a boy!'

'Indeed.' Jason inclined his head, and she could not see
his expression.

Alexandra felt even worse. 'Why did you come here?' she
appealed. 'If—if it's the money . . .'

'What money?' Jason looked at her, but she could not
meet his gaze.

'Supporting me and—and Miss Holland,' she ventured,
and grew hot all over when he left the door to walk slowly
across to her.

'Of course,' he said, halting before her. 'What else could
it be?'

Her eyes darted nervously toward his face, but his
expression was as enigmatic as ever, and she licked at her
dry lips. 'Who—who told you I was working?' she asked.
'If it wasn't Miss Holland, it must have been Manuel. Did—
did you send him here to—to spy on me?'

think I'd do a thing like that?' he probed, a trace
amusement tugging at the corners of his mouth, and it
...ne to her in a flash that he was playing with her now,
like a cat plays with a mouse. Whatever reason had brought
him to London, Estelita must have had something to do
with it, and she must be very sure of him if she dared to
send him here alone.

'How——how is Estelita?' she asked, not really caring, but
wanting to wipe that mocking smile from his face, and his
eyes narrowed.

'I expect she's very well,' he replied at last. 'I don't
know. I haven't seen her for over a week.'

Alexandra stared at him then, but it was useless trying
to read his expression, and with a little cry she turned her
back on him, trying desperately not to jump to conclusions.
But when his hands descended on her shoulders, she didn't
resist him, and the feel of his long length behind her was at
once an agony and a delight.

'Alexandra,' he murmured, and there was no mistaking
the emotion now that thickened his tones. 'Oh, Alexandra,
why did you let me send you away? Have you any idea
what it's been like without you? And when Ricardo told
me you had got a job——'

'Ricardo!'

'Yes, Ricardo. Your Miss Holland was very shrewd. She
didn't write me that you imagined I didn't know about
that letter from Sainte Sœur, or that you had decided not
to come back to San Gabriel. She wrote to Ricardo, knowing full well it was he as much as anybody who had prevented me from riding roughshod over any qualms I might
have had about your youth and marrying you!'

'Jason?' She twisted round in his arms then to stare at
him disbelievingly. 'I——is that true?'

'Would I lie to you?' he demanded, unable to resist the
urge to touch her temples with his lips.

'But——you said we needed time . . .'

'I said *you* needed time,' he muttered, unfastening the

buttons of her blouse with fingers that shook a litt.
by God!' he bent his head to her breast, 'I think I've
you enough, don't you?'

For several minutes, Alexandra could not reply. Wit.
Jason covering her face with kisses and seeking the moist
sweetness of her mouth, she could think of little but him,
and the hardness of his body that even the suede suit
could not disguise. Somehow his waistcoat was unbuttoned,
and the silkiness of his shirt was a sensuous abrasion to
her breasts, while his hands threaded themselves through
her hair and caressed the sensitive skin of her neck and
shoulders. They were hungry for each other, and only the
awareness that Miss Holland might hear them and come to
investigate made Alexandra eventually draw back.

His eyes glazed with emotion, Jason was loath to let her
go, pulling her down on to the couch beside him, im-
prisoning her yielding body beneath his.

'Miss Holland . . .' murmured Alexandra, only half protesting now, and Jason rubbed his tongue across the tip of
her nose.

'I have words to say to Miss Holland later,' he said.
'Somehow I don't think she'll be too surprised to see me.'

Alexandra blinked, trying hard to think coherently.
'You—did you say—I *imagined* you didn't know about the
letter from the convent?' she breathed, and with a sigh, he
rolled to one side of her and took meticulous care over
fastening the buttons of her blouse.

'All right,' he agreed. 'We'll talk. But afterwards . . .'

His eyes left her in no doubt as to his meaning. Un-
guarded, they were warm and intimate, and her heart leapt
in her throat at the realisation that she had aroused those
emotions in him.

'First of all,' he said, unfastening his tie and pulling it
off with evident relief, 'let me tell you about Estelita.'

'What did you mean when you said you hadn't seen her
for a week? You said you only arrived from Rio an hour
ago.'

..' He stroked her mouth with a teasing finger. 'Be
...t, and I'll explain.' She nodded and he went on: 'To
..n with, we'll deal with the letter, shall we? I gather
stelita pretended I knew nothing about it.'

'That's right. She did.' Alexandra's eyes were wide.

'Well, that was—how do they put it?—a bloody lie!'
His lips twitched at her shocked expression. 'My darling,
Ricardo collected my mail that day, not Estelita. She
doesn't have that kind of authority. My God, knowing her
as I do, I would never trust her with my private affairs.'

He paused, and Alexandra recalled again how infuriated
the housekeeper had been when she had found her in
Jason's study.

'Anyway, to continue ... Ricardo collected the mail, as I
say, and naturally he gave the letter to me. If you remember, I had to drive to Puerto Novo to fetch the doctor,
and consequently it was almost supper time before I got
around to reading it.'

Alexandra pressed her lips together. 'Were you very
angry?'

Jason half smiled. 'Do you remember coming downstairs
and finding me in the hall? I'd just read the letter then, and
my thoughts were full of it. Then you said you were leaving,
and I guess my feelings showed.'

Alexandra recalled the occasion very well. 'I thought you
acted strangely,' she murmured reflectively. 'As if—as if
you had expected me to act—differently.'

Jason sighed, tracing the line of her jaw with his lips. 'I
did.' He touched the corner of her mouth. 'After reading
that letter, I would have cut out my tongue before I sent
you away!'

'Jason!'

Her lips parted, and for a long moment there was silence
in the room. Then he stirred himself sufficiently to say:
'Can you not understand? I realised how desperate you
must have been to write that letter, and when you said you
were leaving ... I was shattered.'

'If only you'd told me!'

'If only,' he agreed softly. 'I did try. The n.
were leaving, I came to your room before you w.
knocked long enough. You must have heard me. B.
didn't answer.'

Alexandra propped herself up on one elbow to stare
down at him. 'But the morning I was leaving I was up early,
terribly early. I was down at the stables at first light.'

Jason closed his eyes. 'So that was why——'

'I thought you seemed angry when you came in to breakfast and found me already there.'

'I was.' Jason's fingers curved round her nape. 'I was
sure then you must have heard me. And then when you
shook hands . . .' He squeezed her neck cruelly for a
moment. 'Dear God, you've given me some bad moments!'
He pulled her down to him for a moment and punished her
very satisfactorily, and then he added huskily: 'If I had
known what Estelita had done, I'd have killed her.'

'You never found out?'

'How could I? She wasn't likely to tell me, and you had
forced Miss Holland's hand.'

Alexandra hesitated. 'She—she said she was going to get
you to marry her. She said—even if she had to get pregnant——'

'Oh, God!' Jason buried his face in her hair. 'To get
pregnant you have to do more than cook a man's meals or
do his laundry,' he averred roughly. 'And that's all Estelita
has been doing for me.'

Alexandra's lips trembled. 'She said——'

'I don't care what she said. I'm not saying I haven't
entertained ideas of going to bed with her. I have. But like
I said to you on one famous occasion, I never make those
kind of commitments. To be crude, it's far too easy to drive
into Puerto Novo or Valvedra, if I have to.'

Alexandra's cheeks burned. 'Did you—did you after—
after——'

'After the night of the storm?' he enquired dryly. 'My

..ve no intention of satisfying you on that
you remember, I had other things to worry

mountain lion!' she exclaimed. 'Have you caught

Jason nodded. 'Ricardo shot her the week after you left.
It was an unfortunate affair. One of the men had injured her
on a hunting trip. They'd gone out after geese, and Carlos
was never a marksman. Of course, she had to poach to survive. She must have been in great pain.'

'Poor thing!' Alexandra was moved, although she could
still remember her terror in the canyon.

'Yes,' Jason nodded. 'Anyway, returning to Estelita,
Ricardo had this letter from Miss Holland some time before
he told me. He knew Manuel was going to Rome, so he had
him stop off and see what was happening for himself. When
Manuel confirmed the gist of what Miss Holland had said,
Ricardo decided that much against his better judgment I
would have to be told.'

He shook his head. 'I won't bore you with the details of
what he and I said to one another, or indeed the scene I
had with Estelita. Sufficient to say, she packed her bags at
once, and Ricardo drove her back to Valvedra.'

'Oh, Jason!' Alexandra couldn't help feeling a twinge of
pity for the Spanish woman.

'She'll make out,' Jason replied laconically. 'She has her
brother to care for, and her mother will be coming out of
hospital soon.' He pulled a wry face. 'She could never get
it into her head that I had no intention of marrying again.'

Alexandra's lips parted at this and he bent to cover them
with his own. 'Don't jump to conclusions,' he said. 'I said I
had no intention of marrying again. Unfortunately, that
was before I met you.'

Alexandra linked her arms around his neck. 'And when
did you decide to come back to England?'

'Immediately. But it wasn't that easy. I have an *estancia*
to run, and it's nearing lambing time.' He sighed. 'You see

the trouble you put me to! Like a fool, I jump
plane, take a taxi to Mountsey Square, dump my
with Mrs Beesley—and then face a fiery virago!'

Alexandra's eyes appealed for his understanding
thought—oh, I don't know what I thought. And I was late

'You're even later now,' remarked Jason smugly. 'You'll
probably lose your job. That will save you the necessity of
resigning.'

'You're very sure of me.'

He grimaced. 'Am I? You wouldn't turn me down now,
would you?'

For a moment he had a vulnerability that was disturbingly attractive, and she pressed herself closer to him.
'What do you think?' she breathed, and his mouth sought
the eagerness of hers.

'Well . . .' he said at last, and she could feel the tremor
that went through him as he strove for control, 'Ricardo
can only cope for a few days. Is that enough?'

'Enough?'

'To pack?' he demanded. 'I want to marry you. But not
here. In Puerto Novo, in the church there. Just as soon as
I can get a licence.'

'Oh, but . . .' Alexandra hesitated. 'How long will that
take?'

Jason relaxed. 'Not long. Until then, you'll have to be
content with being my mistress.'

There was another satisfying silence, and then Alexandra
whispered huskily: 'That day—that day in the canyon, you
said you couldn't betray the trust my father had given you,
but—but you suspected he hadn't written to you. Why
didn't you challenge me?'

'Because I wanted you to tell me,' retorted Jason quietly.
'Besides, I still feel I owe your father so much.'

'That's not why——'

'Why I'm marrying you?' he teased. 'Oh, Alexandra, you
know so little about men! Do you honestly think I'd tie myself to any woman out of a debt to her father?'

stroked his cheek. 'I'll make you a good wife,'
.d. 'I know I'm not much good as a cook, but I'm
.cient at cleaning. And I'm willing to learn.'
know you are,' he assured her. 'But for the time being,
.ss Holland's going to come back with us to help you.'

'Miss Holland?'

'Of course. You didn't think I could abandon her, did
you?'

'But how do you—what if she——'

'I phoned,' he admitted half sheepishly. 'But don't blame
her for keeping it to herself. I told her what I'd do if she
let me down a second time.'

Alexandra couldn't find it in her heart to be anything but
grateful to the older woman. 'But she's not a housekeeper,'
she protested, and Jason smiled.

'With luck, her task will be shortlived,' he agreed. 'But
for the present, she'll take the burden of responsibility from
your shoulders. Then, later, when our sons are born . . .'

Alexandra's cheeks burned. 'Our sons!'

'And daughters, too, I hope,' he teased. 'Oh, not immediately—I want you all to myself for the present. But
Luisa and Elena are willing to resume their duties, and
you'll learn to organise them. And besides, we'll need a
good nanny eventually.'

Alexandra could hardly take it in. 'What about Ricardo?'
she ventured. 'Will he accept me?'

'Ricardo has resigned himself to the inevitable,' Jason
responded gently. 'You must forgive his familiarity. We've
known each other a lot of years.'

'He said he knew my father,' said Alexandra remini-
scently, and Jason nodded.

'He did. Like me, he worked in Mexico, too, and when I
discovered how good he was with horses, I offered him the
chance to work for me when I got San Gabriel. I sank
every penny I had in the *estancia*, and I have your father
to thank for that.'

'You mean—you paid for the *estancia* with the n
you earned with my father?'

'Yes,' Jason nodded again.

'Oh!' Alexandra licked her lips, and when he looked
puzzled, she confessed: 'I thought—when you were a
mercenary—I'm sorry, I didn't realise . . .'

Jason understood. 'That money was lost in a speculative
venture in the States,' he agreed. 'There wasn't a lot of it.
The job sickened me after the first few months.'

Alexandra was glad. 'So you and Ricardo went to Santa
Vittoria.'

'Yes. Ricardo—and Manuel. He was just a boy then.'

'He still is,' said Alexandra at once. 'How could you think
I . . .'

'A man in love thinks crazy things,' retorted Jason pas-
sionately. 'God, the torment you've put me through!'

'Miss Holland told me you—you put me to bed the night
of the storm,' murmured Alexandra inconsequently, seeing
the beads of sweat start on his forehead.

'I did.' He closed his eyes in remembered agony. 'That
was when I deluded myself I could handle the situation.'

'So that was why you were so—so casual in the kitchen
afterwards.'

'Casual? Was I?' He grinned. 'You saw how casual I was
a few minutes later.'

Alexandra wriggled closer to him. 'I can't wait to go
back to San Gabriel. I've hated London. I've hated being
apart from you. When can we leave?'

'Soon,' he promised huskily. 'But don't worry, I'll never
leave you again.'

Alexandra sighed. 'You know what I want to do,' she
murmured dreamily. 'Go with you on the trail—next time
you round up the horses.'

'When the snow has gone?' he asked lazily, and laughed
at her astonished face. 'Oh, yes, we get a little snow. Not a
lot, but some. Why? What are you planning to do? Look

chestnut mare? There's no need. I got her back, safe
sound.'

'You did?'

He nodded, a wry smile crossing his face. 'Actually,
perhaps safe and sound was the wrong description. She's in
foal. I'll let you choose the name when her time is due, shall
I?'

'The black stallion!' exclaimed Alexandra ruefully. 'My
downfall and my salvation!'

'No—mine,' Jason corrected her softly, and when Miss
Holland came to find out if everything was well, she tiptoed
away again, unseen.

The Warrender Saga

The most frequently requested series of Harlequin Romances . . . Mary Burchell's Warrender Saga

A Song Begins   The Curtain Rises
The Broken Wing   Song Cycle
Child of Music   Music of the Heart
         Unbidden Melody
      Remembered Serenade
      When Love Is Blind

Each complete novel is set in the exciting world of music and opera, spanning the years from the meeting of Oscar and Anthea in *A Song Begins* to his knighthood in *Remembered Serenade*. These nine captivating love stories introduce you to a cast of characters as vivid, interesting and delightful as the glittering, exotic locations. From the tranquil English countryside to the capitals of Europe— London, Paris, Amsterdam—the Warrender Saga will sweep you along in an unforgettable journey of drama, excitement and romance.

...most frequently requested
Harlequin Romance series

A Song Begins

#1508 *Child of Music*

#1100 *The Broken Wing*

#1587 *Music of the Heart*

#1244 *When Love Is Blind*

#1767 *Unbidden Melody*

#1405 *The Curtain Rises*

#1834 *Song Cycle*

#1936 *Remembered Serenade*

Complete and r̶...
this coupon today̶...

Remember when a good love story made you feel like holding hands?

The wonder of love is timeless. Once discovered, love remains, despite the passage of time. Harlequin brings you stories of true love, about women the world over—women like you.

Harlequin Romances with the Harlequin magic...

Recapture the sparkle of first love...relive the joy of true romance...enjoy these stories of love today.

Six new novels every month— wherever paperbacks are sold.

Do you have a favorite Harlequin author? Then here is an opportunity you must not miss!